Dedication

This book is dedicated to my wife Bonnie, my true soul mate.

Order this book online at www.trafford.com/07-1496
or email orders@trafford.com

Most Trafford titles are also available at major online book retailers.

Edited by: Leeann Womble Smith

Cover Design Artwork: Debbie Culler

Designed by: Ralph Stanley Hazen

© Copyright 2007 Ralph Stanley Hazen.

All rights reserved. No part of this publication may be reproduced, stored in a retrieval system, or transmitted, in any form or by any means, electronic, mechanical, photocopying, recording, or otherwise, without the written prior permission of the author.

Note for Librarians: A cataloguing record for this book is available from Library and Archives Canada at www.collectionscanada.ca/amicus/index-e.html

Printed in Victoria, BC, Canada.

ISBN: 978-1-4251-3767-0

We at Trafford believe that it is the responsibility of us all, as both individuals and corporations, to make choices that are environmentally and socially sound. You, in turn, are supporting this responsible conduct each time you purchase a Trafford book, or make use of our publishing services. To find out how you are helping, please visit www.trafford.com/responsiblepublishing.html

Our mission is to efficiently provide the world's finest, most comprehensive book publishing service, enabling every author to experience success. To find out how to publish your book, your way, and have it available worldwide, visit us online at www.trafford.com/10510

www.trafford.com

North America & international
toll-free: 1 888 232 4444 (USA & Canada)
phone: 250 383 6864 ♦ fax: 250 383 6804
email: info@trafford.com

The United Kingdom & Europe
phone: +44 (0)1865 722 113 ♦ local rate: 0845 230 9601
facsimile: +44 (0)1865 722 868 ♦ email: info.uk@trafford.com

10 9 8 7 6 5 4 3 2

Acknowledgements

I wish to thank my wife, Bonnie, for her understanding And support while writing this novel. I also want to thank my family and friends as well. A special thanks to my Editor, Lee Ann Womble Smith for her perseverance and tenacity in getting it done right. Congratulations to Book Cover Artist, Debbie Culler, who performed an outstanding job on the artwork. Without the support of those individuals, this novel wouldn't have happened.

Bannerstone

Ralph Stanley Hazen

One

The clouds seemed to be parting and rolling, black as coal. "That's a typical Kansas spring storm brewing," thinking to my self as I drove west toward the Colorado border. Soon as it gets hot the tornado weather starts.

I rolled the window down on my old 1948 Ford pickup. The new 1956 pickups came out a few months ago and they are pretty to look at but they're too darn expensive for me.

Besides, this old truck and I have been through a lot together.

You could smell the strong sweet odor of rain in the air. Looking off to the southwest, a line of black rough edged clouds was moving across the horizon. Normally, I wouldn't be out here in this flat, wide open country with a storm brewing like this one, especially without a deep road ditch to get into.

But, I got this feeling, call it intuition. This same feeling has hit me before and it's never been wrong. It's time for me to meet Taza again. It's been about six months since her last visit. The time between visits has been getting longer and I see her for a shorter period each visit.

There is change coming and a fear of something I don't quite understand. It's a feeling of losing someone very close to you. It's tough to explain, anyway, I can't do anything about it so, what the heck.

Ahead, I could see the outline of hills where Taza and I had met last time.

The dust was boiling up under the truck and some was even coming in the window. I've got an idea that if this storm closes in, I might wish I'd have a storm cellar to get in.

Finally, I got to the old sandstone fencepost pile off to my right. This is where I turn off the main road to the left. It looks like a cow path, but if you look close you can see deep ruts running alongside the road. This is where the wagon tracks start. These wagon tracks were made back when the early settlers were going west.

In the spring when the frost comes out of the ground, this prairie grass gets like a sponge. I guess those heavy loaded wagons must have left some really deep ruts. It's incredible to still be able to see those ruts after this length of time.

This road leads up to a small trickling spring about a quarter of a mile straight ahead. The spring comes right out of the rocks at the back of the box canyon.

The old Oxhide Trail runs close by here. It connects the Chisholm Trail and the Santa Fe Trails. Guess that's why the wagons would come up here in the box canyon to make camp.

Not too many places around where you can find water, especially if you got horses and cattle to water.

I pulled my truck into the box canyon. A lightning strike hit a lonesome tree up on the rim of the canyon. The thunder boomed. You could feel the whole truck shake. I was glad to be in the canyon just in case there was a twister around.

I drove up near the back wall of the canyon and shut off the engine and pushed the door open. Stepping out on the running board, I caught a glimpse of a dark object descending down and moving toward me. As the lightning struck, you could see an outline of the P.S.V. That's a "Planetary Space Vehicle."

Every time I see this thing I am totally amazed that it even exists. Taza has never allowed me to board; she say's the strong magnetic fields are dangerous to be around unless you wear proper equipment.

She wears a wide belt made of a special anti-gravitational material. She say's it is made from a trace element found only on her home Planet, Junlk.

It's a planet hidden from Earth's view by other planets and due to its small size and unique makeup of elements, it's well hidden.

As the P.S.V moved within 30 yards, it hovered about 10 feet above the ground. Three legs about 4 inches in diameter with round dish shaped pads, slowly extended at a wide angle out of the rim section of the vehicle. When it was about 4 feet off the ground, the legs moved on down to support the vehicle in a level plane. The ground was really uneven and rocky.

No noise came from the vehicle as it sat like a huge whale nosed dish. A heavy blue haze exhausted from large round holes around the rim as the magnetic engines began to slow.

My heart was pounding, I don't know if it's the awesomeness of the craft or the anticipation of seeing Taza again.

The craft sat motionless and silent. At that moment, a large round tube extended out from the bottom and extended slowly down till it touched the ground.

As it touched, the side of the tube rotated open. A blue light highlighted the silhouette of a tall, thin figure standing in the opening.

The figure started towards me, I knew that walk; it was Taza. She moved like a marble on silk. Her red hair blew around her face as she approached. I walked up to meet her.

I threw my arms around her. We held each other tight and kissed. Her lips were hot. They felt like a blow torch.

I held her tight against my body. I could feel her heart beating, pounding against my chest. I realized how much I missed this woman and how I wanted to spend a lot of time with her.

She spoke in a soft whisper, "I've missed you so very, very much." I replied with a swollen lump in my throat, "I didn't think you Junlk"s showed emotion."

She looked up at me with her beautiful emerald green tearful eyes saying, "My father has passed on to another dimension and time."

I held her tight against my body as she wept quietly. I had met her father during their last visit which was only about six months ago. He seemed healthy as a horse then. Maybe he had an accident or something?

"Taza, how did your father die?" She answered while her head lay on my shoulder. "We were on an exploratory mining mission to Plura, a planet beyond the Kana Asteroid belt in the Yura galaxy."

"We had spent 2 days on Plura when we experienced solar storms from the Sun."

"They were starting to extend extraordinarily close to Plura and were creating problems with our ships magnetic engines and guidance systems."

"Father had taken ill the day we left but I thought the illness may have been due to radiation exposure."

"He had experienced high exposure from a solar flare while gathering mineral samples on the Plura surface."

"Father should have recovered completely after receiving medical treatment for radiation exposure, but he never responded."

"He only became weaker each day till he had no choice but to move to another time dimension."

As I listened to Taza tell about the circumstances of her father's death; I felt deeply sorry for Taza.

"Taza, I'm really sorry to hear of your father's death." Taza pulled away quickly, looking at me directly as if studying my face.

"Our people don't experience death as you know it. When we reach a time our bodies can no longer function, we move to a different time dimension by means of a molecular regenerator accelerator."

"Each group or family, as you consider it, all gather eventually at the same time dimension and continue to enjoy each others presence and association. So as you see, we're only apart for a short time."

"We have been working on a multi light synchronizer for communication to various time dimensions but have not been successful in establishing two way communications."

"He had always been there when I had a question or concern, a father, and my friend."

"I miss him so very much."

We stood together quietly as if saying our last respects.

Taza reached into the breast pocket of her suit, removing a small velvet bag. She held out her hand to mine, I felt the soft velvet against the palm of my hand, I closed my hand tightly.

Taza spoke softly. "It was my fathers wish that you have this."

I opened my hand; the velvet bag had a flap covering the opening. Pulling the flap back, I removed a black stone from the bag. There was a hole in the center of the 3 inch long stone where a leather necklace strap was tied. The stone was crescent shaped in length and approximately one inch thick.

Holding the stone, I felt warmth I'd never experienced before. Taza took the stone from my hand and hung the leather necklace around my neck. The stone hung just below my breast bone.

The warmth I felt when I touched the stone with my hand was now penetrating through my entire body. I felt a lofty, strong feeling in my mind.

I closed my eyes; I could see energy streaks inside my eyelids, flashing like lighting.

"What is this Taza?" Taza spoke softly. "This stone is called, "BANNERSTONE."

"This stone was worn by the ancients who were the first of our people to observe planet Earth."

"This occurred 9605 earth years past."

"It has power even beyond our understanding today."

"It is recorded, the Bannerstone was given to the ancients by the Great Spirit; very similar to the way your ancients received your ten commandments."

"The stone is a communication device."

"It has multiple functions and can store data and direct or channel information to other sources."

"The warmth you felt is basically an ejection of free electrons as it process information."

"The uniqueness of the Bannerstone is that it has your personal biological features programmed internally."

"Only you can activate its use."

"When you removed it from its protective pouch and touched the stone, it ran a scan of your internal spirit or soul, as you earthlings refer to it."

"Wearing it around your neck places it specifically in the central portion of your body where it is activated only by your conscience or sub conscience brain waves."

"The wearing of the stone gives access to a data bank of understanding and knowledge much beyond our understanding."

"It guided our ancients to find planet earth and start the education and training of your ancient civilizations in mathematics and science."

As I listened to Taza, I felt completely numb. I knew what she was telling me was the truth, but why me?

"Taza, why did your father choose me to have this Bannerstone?" Taza reached out and took hold of my hand saying," Father knew when he met you for the first time that you were the chosen one."

"That's why he took the necessary biological information the first time you met him."

"Remember when you pricked your finger on his jacket when you shook hands at our parting visit, she asked?"

"I must tell you, that was a little less than totally honest but it was necessary that your genes and your spirit were properly joined, or in other words, you were ready for the task ahead of you."

"This information was also programmed into the Bannerstone."

"He knew that you were capable of handling the responsibility and challenge of this unique power and that you would use this power for the good of mankind, and all kind."

"Knowledge is the foundation and the superstructure of all civilizations."

"Life, like a comet, born bright and heading full speed through the universe, but like life, gone too soon." "Knowledge and experience once discovered; no one shall ever be the same again."

I stood thinking where this knowledge might lead me. Taza leaned forward and kissed me on the cheek. I looked into her beautiful green eyes.

She spoke softly, "my love, I must be leaving, but I will be as close as your thoughts."

I replied, "GOD speed", and I pulled her close to me and held her and whispered, "I'll miss you terribly."

Taza turned and walked back to the waiting P.S.V. As she entered the loading tube she turned. A smile was showing sweet and clear. The tube rotated and disappeared up into the craft.

The magnetic engines energized and the craft was gone in a blink of an eye.

Two

I walked back to my old pickup truck pulling my shirt collar close to my neck. The rain was really starting to come down. I opened the truck door and slid in. The door slammed hard, shutting with a clank as the window rattled in the door. I hit the starter, the engine fired up.

Turning the truck around was a challenge as I backed up into a brush pile stacked along the old cow path road; jocking back and forth finally getting the truck headed in the other direction. A big Russian thistle, better known as a tumble weed, caught under the truck and when I pulled forward, you could hear the dragging. The heck with it I thought, and continued down the road.

That tumble weed must have hung on for five miles. Then I heard a "whump".

The tumble weed had broken free from the truck and now could carry on its life of rolling around where ever the wind decided to blow it.

I wondered if life is something like that. When you don't have a plan on what you want to do with the rest of your life.

What ever comes along, you go that way, then something else comes along, and then you go that way.

Although I do believe that God has a plan for everyone already written in the book of life. I couldn't help but feel that by getting this Bannerstone, my life would never be the same.

The rain continued to fall steadily. The wind against the windshield ran tiny rivers down the glass as the single windshield wiper worked desperately to keep the windshield dry enough for me to see the road.

Only the dim dash lights illuminated the inside of the truck.

Reaching up, I touched the Bannerstone which hung around my neck. It felt warm and calming, yet somewhat mysterious.

The headlights lit up the road like two candles. I would be coming to the turn in the road soon.

The truck slowed and finally could see the sandstone fence post pile in front of me and I turned right onto the main road.

I was glad we didn't have a twister tonight; those black clouds can pop out a tornado in a heartbeat. The rain was letting up but it had rained enough to settle the dust on the road and put some water in the shallow ditches.

The truck headlights lit up the Ellinwood city limit sign. Looking at the dim lit dash clock, it was showing midnight.

All the town street lights were out. There had been a power failure.

My headlights lit up a billboard lying flat out in the middle of the street. Turning the truck down main street, I got a glimpse of a flashing light. It was the town fire truck.

It was parked at a 45 degree angle in the middle of the street. I pulled up to the fire truck and jumped out quickly.

"Gary, what's going on here?" A voice came back," Where have you been?"

"We had us a good old Kansas twister here tonight." My heart dropped, I knew everyone in town, being born and raised here.

Ellinwood is a small town and when something happens to anyone in town, it affects everyone.

"Gary, how much damage did it do?"

"Was anyone hurt?" Gary answered," we're not sure."

"It knocked out all the power in town including the telephone system and the R.E.A (Rural Electrification Authority) guys are working on the power now to kill all the live lines that are down."

"I saw their truck down at the substation about fifteen minutes after the twister hit."

"It hit the east part of town the worst." Gary's voice was quivering as he spoke.

"Hell, that's where I live," I hollered out loud; "I'm going on over there."

Gary yelled back as I was getting into my truck, "watch out for hot power lines down."

I dropped the transmission into reverse, scraping gears as I popped the clutch and spun tires going around the corner, driving as fast as I possibly could toward my house.

The next block, I turned right and I could see a house roof lying in the middle of the street. Standing along side the roof I could just make out three figures.

I pulled the truck up close, the headlights lit up their faces. It was Charlie Schmidt, his wife Nora and his daughter Lee.

"Charlie, are you alright?" Charlie answered in a slow non emotional voice. "Well, everything's pretty good, none of us is hurt, we were in the storm cellar when the twister hit."

"The house ain't too good a shape though, looks like it's totaled."

Charlie laid his hand on my shoulder saying, "how's your place?"

"Did you get much damage?" I answered, "I don't know, I just got back in town and I was heading our there when I saw you."

"Do you mind if we ride over there with you, Charlie asked?" "I'd like to check on Mom and things at the old home place."

"Sure Charlie, I think we can all squeeze in."

I leaned over and opened the passenger side door. Charlie's daughter Lee slide in next to me, his wife Nora and then Charlie squeezed us all up tight and slammed the truck door hard. I think I know what sardines in a can must feel like.

Lee was packed up tight against me; she slid her skirt up above her knees so she could straddle the gear shift lever.

I reached for the gear shift knob and dropped the truck into low gear.

Lee and I had gone through school together in the same grade. Our senior year we dated the whole year.

Don't really know why we quit going together. I guess she scared me off because she was getting really serious about us having a permanent relationship.

I had college to think of and knew I'd have trouble supporting myself and didn't want to put her through that kind of life. I guess I loved her too much to do that to her.

I put my hand on the gear shift knob to shift into second gear. Lee laid her hand over mine. She nudged me with her elbow saying, "mind if I help you shift?" I answered shyly, "no, not at all."

It was embarrassing due to the parents in the truck. The engine reached R.P.M., I shifted into third gear. Lee's legs tightened against the gear shift. I thought for a moment that I better shift back to second gear, but she pulled the gear shift on down into third gear.

Her hand tightened on mine. I started getting nervous, my face was hot and I knew my face was blood red. It's a good thing it was dark in the truck. I then realized Lee was doing this for darned orneriness just to embarrass me.

We turned the next corner; debris was scattered across the street and a big cottonwood tree was lying across the roof of Bill Elder's house.

It looked like the twister's path came down this block. I slowed to a stop. Charlie was the first out of the truck.

"Charlie, watch out for hot power lines, I hollered." I turned to Lee and Nora, "Stay in the truck, we're going to see if anyone needs help."

Charlie and I walked through the rubble. I caught a muffled noise. "Charlie", I hollered, "I think someone is under this debris."

The walls of a house had been pushed in and lying nearly flat on the ground. The noise seemed to come from under the long flat section. I was down on the ground and sliding on my stomach to see if I could get under the debris.

"It's too dark, we need a flashlight."

Charlie yelled back, "tough luck, we left ours back in the storm cellar."

"No, I got it, Lee shouted, "Mama brought the flashlight with her." Lee had got out of the truck and was walking towards us. "Hurry up", I shouted, "there's someone under here."

Lee was picking her way through the debris. I could see a flash of light cutting back and forth as Lee approached.

The flashlight beam suddenly went up in the air. Lee had tripped over something and she hit the ground like a ton of bricks. I heard her "umph", as she fell.

"Are you alright?" There was a long silence. Then slowly Lee answered, "I think so, I'm not sure."

"My dress is caught on a nail or something." Before I could answer, I heard a loud rip. I could see the light moving toward me again.

Lee was crawling on her hands and knees, moving slowly picking her way through the splintered wood and debris.

"Lee, are you really OK?"

"You really hit the ground hard." Lee answered, "Yea, I'm OK, but I think I left half of my dress back there." Then I heard it again. A low tone groan came from under the flattened wall section off to my right.

"It's over this way". Lee and I pulled and pushed lumber and pieces of door and windows out of the way. This is a mess, I thought as we slid another wall section sideways.

This next section was off the ground just enough that I couldn't get under it, but I reached back as far as I could but I couldn't feel anything.

Lee pushed me aside. "Let me try, I'm smaller than you," Lee said, as she slide past me.

I realized what she meant when she said she left half of her dress back there on a nail. I held the flashlight while she pushed and squirmed through the wreckage.

She yelled back, "I've found someone."

"I've got hold of their leg."

"Push on me, Lee pleaded; "I need to squeeze between these rafters." I reached under the wall as far as I could, only just to touch Lee's foot. I shouted back to Lee, "I'm going to turn around and push on you with my feet."

I slid out on my shoulder and spun around grasping hold of a two by four board that was part of the wall section and I thrust my legs and body forward under the flattened wall.

My feet slid past Lee's feet and stopped abrupt against her butt. I felt her move forward.

"That's good," she replied, "I've got through the rafters and I going to crawl on in." There was dead silence.

"Lee what's going on?" Lee answered back in a shaken voice. "Shine the light back here."

I squirmed around pushing debris out of the way as much as I could. I finally got a clear beam of light back to where Lee was at.

I held the light on Lee, she shouted, "My God, It's the little Govia girl." I shouted back to Lee, "Is she conscious?"

Lee answered back in a tearful shaken voice, "no, I can't even feel a heart beat and I don't think she's breathing." "God I think she's dead!"

"Oh Rolf, Rolf, help me, Lee said."

My heart was pounding like a trip hammer and adrenalin was pumping through my veins. I slid out from under the wall section.

Charlie and I grabbed under the rafters and with a mighty jerk, we felt the wall move up. In a desperation cry, "Get out of there, I shouted."

Lee started backing out dragging the little lifeless girl behind her. My knees were locked and Charlie was standing and starting to shake all over.

I stood there not knowing how long we could hold this weight.

My thoughts went to the Bannerstone hanging around my neck. It was hot lying against my chest. "Charlie, I'll hold this up, pull Lee out."

My knees stopped shaking as I held the roof section up.

Lee was in tears and she had the little girls dress belt clinched in her hand and tugging to pull her out.

As they cleared from under the debris, I dropped the wall section. It fell with a horrible crashing sound.

"Pick up the flashlight there on the ground and shine it so I can see her face."

Lee was right; there was no sign of breathing. I put my ear to her small chest, there was no heart beat.

I laid my hands on each side of her head, thinking, oh God, this little girl needs to live and her life has just begun. My thoughts moved to what Taza had told me about the Bannerstone and the power to communicate with a greater being, maybe the Great Spirit.

I concentrated, pushing my thoughts up through the top of my brain. The Bannerstone was really getting hot; it felt like a hot coal lying on my chest.

I felt a surge of energy flow from my body through my hands to the little girls head.

Her eyes opened, she looked up wide eyed. She began to cry. "Mama, Mama, where's my mama?"

Lee grabbed her up and held her close to her chest and hugged her tightly. "Your mama is around here someplace, you need to help us find her, OK?"

The little girl looked up with tearful eyes and answered softly. "OK, because I know my mama needs me."

I asked her if she hurt anyplace. She answered, "I don't think so; can we find mama now?"

"Yea, I answered, let's go find your mama."

We started back to the truck and there was Nora. She had left the truck and was picking her way through the debris to find out what was going on.

She was asking all kinds of questions about what had happened. Charlie was filling her in on the details. Both Lee and I hesitated on saying very much because we really didn't know ourselves.

Nora said, "I'll take the child back to the truck."

"Fine, I said, but keep an eye on her; she's had a really bad time here and I hope her mom shows up soon."

"Charlie, let's you and I look through the rest of this rubble." Lee abruptly said, "Well, I'm going with you guys."

"OK, I answered, but watch out for nails sticking out of those boards; I've already stepped on one."

"I'm not a child anymore Rolf," Lee snorted back in a half discussed voice. I snickered a little saying, "Yea, I've noticed." Lee turned toward me and looked me directly in the eyes. "Well it's about damn time."

Charlie broke in, let's get to looking, there might be someone else out here that needs help."

We moved through the debris of one house site to another. I could start to see the direction the twister took. "It looks like it touched down about Bill Elders house and went back up on the other side of Inman's place."

"What do you think Charlie?"

"Yea, Charlie answered, I think so, but we probably need to go on out of town to see if it touched down again."

"Charlie, you and Nora take the truck and the little Govia girl and drive over to their Grandmother's house and see where her mom and dad are at."

Charlie answered, "That's a good idea."

"Lee and I will keep looking around here."

Three

I heard the truck crank up and Charlie grind the transmission gears as he headed up the next street. Lee and I worked our way up the street looking through each house or what was remaining standing.

In this area only roofs seemed to be blown off. People were starting to pop up everywhere. Most of the people were coming out of their storm cellars or their neighbor's cellars. I figured I must have got into town about twenty minutes after it hit.

"It looks like we might as well walk back toward the way we came Lee; I don't see anymore major damage here."

As we walked along, Lee started laughing; she had shined her flashlight on a pair of purple panties hanging on a picket fence. She said, "Those are Mrs. Ashcraft panties; you know, the piano teacher and she also plays organ in our church."

"How do you know those are Mrs. Ashcraft's Panties?"

"Well, Lee said, last Sunday as I was walking into the ladies room at church, I heard a loud noise and as I turned around, Mrs. Ashcraft was in one of the stalls and had dropped her Bible on the floor, probably fell asleep reading it."

"Well, when she tried to grab up her Bible, her panties fell to the floor."

"I could see them as plain as day under the stall door and I'd recognize Mrs. Ashcraft's shoes anyplace."

"No one has worn those kinds of shoes since the thirties and those are her purple lace panties."

"Well, let her find them tomorrow because I don't want to deliver them to her. I'm sure everyone is going to be out trying to recover what they can."

Lee agreed, grabbing my hand as we walked back toward my place.

We walked along the sidewalk. I couldn't help from thinking about Taza. I felt about half guilty holding hands with Lee and knowing my real love was Taza. Under the circumstances, Lee had been through a lot tonight and I felt a real closeness towards her.

Just ahead I could see the outline of my house. My heart was in my throat. We got closer; I started breathing a bit of relief.

Lee spoke softly," Rolf it looks like the twister missed your house."

"Yea, it looks like the good Lord has blessed me again." We walked up to the house and stood by the front yard iron gate.

"Lee, this house was built by my Grandpa Noll."

"He liked working with stone, so he built the whole house out of river rock including the rock wall around the yard." "It's a large old house, but it sure is cozy."

The iron gate swung open with a hair rising screech. "I guess I need to oil that gate one of these days." Lee nodded in agreement.

Lee walked up the rock sidewalk ahead of me to the front porch. She stopped when she reached the front door.

"What do you think about us sitting here in the porch swing for a while?"

"I feel like I need to sit down."

"Sure, I said, I could definitely sit for a while myself." We sat down in the old oak swing. It popped and cracked then settled in to handle the load of the two of us. We swung gently back and forth, the cool damp morning air held all kinds of smells.

The old time roses grew like a bouquet and were really outdoing themselves. The dark red color decorated the inside of the rock wall that surrounded the front yard. It's too dark yet to see the roses but the fragrance in the air helped you visualize them in your mind.

I turned to Lee, "you know I got an old shirt and a pair of blue jeans that I outgrew a while back, they just might fit you."

Lee answered,"ya, I need to put something on, this dress is ripped ever which way and with it getting daylight soon, I'd hate for the whole town to be talking about me instead of the twister."

I opened the front door, Lee went in first. "You know Lee; I agree with you about that dress, it doesn't cover much."

I love to tease that girl. I went upstairs to see what I could find for Lee to wear. She followed me up the stairs and into the spare bedroom. It had been a while since the room had been opened up and it carried somewhat of a musty smell.

Lee pointed this out to me quickly. "Don't you ever air this room?" She went to the window, as she leaned over to raise the window; her torn dress parted exposing her long leg up to her white panties. I grabbed the first pair of old Levi's I could find in the closet.

"Lee, get these darn blue jeans on." I was actually trembling. Whether she intended to or not, she shook me up. Lee turned around; she had a little smile on her face saying, "can't handle it huh?"

I knew right then she did it on purpose. "Come on get your clothes changed, here's one of my old white shirts."

"I can't even button the collar at the neck anymore, it should fit you." She started unbuttoning her dress. I spun around and closed the door behind me.

Lee was a beautiful young lady and she knew it. If she didn't come on to me so hard, I could get to like her again, even date her. We used to have it hot for each other when we were in high school.

I waited outside the bedroom. It seemed like forever. What takes a woman so long to put on a shirt and pants? The door opened. Lee's hair was combed, pulled back, and she looked great in those old blue jeans and white shirt. She had the sleeves rolled up and the three top buttons open.

"Except for the darn waist so big, these jeans fit pretty well."

"Ya", I said, surprisingly enough, you do fill them out well."

"It's getting daylight now, so we probably need to walk through town to see what damage the twister did last night." "Let's go," Lee responded.

We walked down the street; Lee reached over and clasp my hand in hers. She asked, "You know, I've been thinking about what happened last night."

"The way we got that little Govia girl out from under that house wall."

"I still don't know how you and Dad lifted that heavy wall section and then you revived that little girl? I know she was not breathing and didn't have a heart beat when we got her out."

I looked directly into her big green eyes. "I really don't know either but I'd just as soon you didn't tell anyone about it." Lee questioned, "Why not, you're a real hero."

"No Lee, you're the real hero; you crawled in under that flatted house and pulled that little girl out; you saved her life."

"Rolf, let's just say, "We", worked together to get her out."

"Ya, but no details, OK?" Lee agreed.

We strolled toward main street. Charlie pulled up next to us in the pickup truck. Charlie hollered," Where have you been?"

"We've been driving around town for an hour trying to find you two." I answered back, "how's the little Govia girl?" Charlie came back quickly, "she's doing fine, but I think she got a pretty hard knock on the head."

"She's talking about seeing herself lying under that house and then seeing a bright light and a swirling tunnel she walked through and she said she seen her dog Skippy that died last year; really spooky I'd say."

Lee spoke up, "I've heard of people that died and have been revived and have experienced things like that." Lee looked at me trying to get me to back up her statement," but I'm sure that never happened to her because she seemed OK when we found her, right Rolf?"

"Oh yea," I commented. All the time I was thinking, I sure hope Lee can keep this reviving incident to herself. I don't want to raise any attention to myself because I haven't figured out this Bannerstone thing yet.

People tend to get carried away and crazy when they think someone among them has a special power or just different from them. Nora leaned across Charlie saying, "Leona Govia was at her mothers house and they were ready to send out a search party to hunt for their daughter."

"They sure were happy to see her, they cried and things really got emotional."

"They said to tell you both thanks and God bless you."

"I'm just glad she was alright I answered." Lee and I crawled into the bed of the pickup because Charlie and Nora were taking up the front seat. We'd no more than got in and sit down when Charlie shot the gas to my old pickup. He drove this truck like it was his.

I'd never ridden in the back of my own truck; man was it hard riding. Charlie was running over everything in the street; limbs, garbage can lids, and pieces of lumber. I beat on the top of the cab. "Where are you going in such a hurry", I shouted to Charlie. "Just sit down and hold on," was his response, "you'll know soon enough."

I had just sat down and slid back to lean against the truck bed and cab when I felt the Bannerstone getting warm against my chest. At that moment, I saw a vision flash through my mind and across my eyes.

"Charlie", I shouted," slow down," there's a tree lying across the road just over this hill!" Charlie slammed on the brakes.

The truck slide about half sideways and came to a stop just over the hill top.

Sure as shooting, there was a big cottonwood tree lying across the street. It was exactly like I visualized.

Charlie threw the door open on the truck and swung out standing on the running board. "Damn," I'm glad you seen that, I'd have plowed right into that darn tree at full throttle."

Charlie slid back in the truck and started it up. "We got to go back around the block and through the alley to see if we can get to our house."

Lee leaned over to me and in a low voice, "how did you know a tree was in the road?"

"Neither you nor I could have seen that tree because we were both sitting down in the floor of the pickup bed." Lee grabbed the front of my shirt and pulled me up next to her, nose to nose. She said, "I want to know the truth, the whole damn truth, what's going on with you?"

I was starting to panic. Should I tell Lee about the Bannerstone? She'll wonder where I got it, then I'll have to tell her about Taza, then she'll probably think I'm a nut and not believe me anyway.

"No not now," I quickly responded, "Later, but not now."

"Don't wait too long," Lee grumbled, "I'm not a patient person."

"I know, I know, but right now, I think your dad wants to see what can be salvaged from your house or what's left of it."

Charlie had picked his way through the downed trees and up the alley to the back of their property. He'd run over enough trash and debris with my truck that it was a wonder we didn't have a flat tire or a torn off muffler.

Charlie brought the truck to a screeching halt. He flung open the truck door and was out in the alley with his hands on his hips, shaking his head and shouting in a loud voice. "Well Hell, it flattened my workshop and I bet it ruined my brand new DeWalt Radial arm saw I just got for my birthday." Nora spoke up." You shouldn't be worrying about your darned tools; you should be worrying where you're going to lay your head because this house ain't no more".

I lay my hand on Charlie's shoulder, "Charlie, you know I got this big house and only me in it, I'd sure appreciate some company and you'd be close to your house when you start to rebuild it."

Nora turned to me saying, "That's a mighty generous offer Rolf, but we couldn't put our problems on you."

I answered, "Nora, that's the darndest thing I've ever heard."

"You know I've eaten more meals at your house than I did at mine when I was growing up."

"Let's say we're just going to even up the feed bag bill." "What do you say, let's salvage what we can, load it in the pickup and haul it over to my house."

"We can put stuff in the garage too if you need to."

Charlie spoke up, "We sure do appreciate this Rolf, your Mom and Dad would really be proud of you if they were living."

Four

Over the next several hours we picked up everything from dishes to old pictures and everything imaginable. We must have made three dozen trips. The garage was about half full and one of the spare rooms upstairs and the attic was packed.

Surprising enough, we found most of the important things like the family Bible, pictures and things that couldn't be replaced. The twister had virtually ripped the roof clean off and dropped it in the street. One side of the house looked as though someone had taken a wrecking ball to it.

The rain that followed did a lot of damage to the things inside the house; it must have been a real frog choker.

Charlie and Nora took the large bedroom downstairs. Lee took the guest bedroom upstairs and I took back my old bedroom which was at the end of the hall next to the bathroom.

I walked into my old room, plopped down and settled back against the headboard of my old cannonball bed. I started thinking, you know Lee's Mom is a really great cook and I've really got tired of my own cooking. This might be like old times when Mom used to be here.

This room sure brings back a lot of good old memories. I looked around the room and zeroed in on my telescope and stand that was still positioned in front of the window. I can remember when I used to look more at Lee's house than I did at the stars.

I also remember one hot summer night when I was observing the Milky Way; I had my window wide open, the sweet smell of yellow clover filled the air.

I had just swung the telescope toward the East horizon when I picked up a bright light moving directly towards me. The light seemed to be moving up and down.

I had been watching aircraft coming out of Fort Riley Air force base before but this was totally different.

I watched for about five minutes through the telescope. As it got closer, I swung the telescope out of the way and watched it through the open window.

I remember the whole thing like it happened yesterday. I couldn't believe what I was seeing. The object had different colors coming off it and it seemed to circle the town. I'd see it for a while and then I wouldn't see it.

Then all of a sudden it looked like Fourth of July fireworks display. Lights were moving in all directions.

I remember it moved away from town and suddenly stopped in mid air and slowly descended to the ground with the circle of lights still shining.

I ran downstairs, out the gate and to the garage. I jumped on my old Henderson bicycle and tore out towards where I had seen the lights.

I even remember the moon was about three quarters full so I could see pretty well where I was going; I thought.

I had that old bike wound out and I was moving fast down the dirt road.

Then I felt the front wheel drop and a "Thud". The wheel hit the bottom of a ditch which had washed across the road.

All I could think of for that split second was where that ditch came from. Then I remember flying through the air over the handlebars and my head hitting something solid.

I can still hear that dull thud and then I was out cold.

My head was heavy and things looked foggy. I started waking up like from a really sound sleep. I remember looking up, my eyes focused on some shiny crinkled cover over me.

There stood three people, dressed really different and looking down at me.

I thought maybe I was still dreaming. One of them spoke, asking if I was injured and if I had pain.

I could hear them talking but no one moved their mouth. Then I realized that I didn't hear what they said, but I knew what they said. I was convinced that I was still dreaming.

Then a beautiful red haired girl with the most beautiful green eyes leaned down over me and looked closely into my eyes.

This was my first meeting with Taza. She spoke in a soft voice; "You're back from a deep unconscious state."

She placed her warm hands on each side of my face. I could feel my heart beat in my throat.

That was the last thing I remembered until I woke up laying on the ground beside my old bicycle.

Ya, this room really does bring back a lot of old memories.

Well, I better hit the sack. I feel like I've been up for a week. Moving and carrying furniture is not my idea of a way to spend a day, but, it was a very good feeling to be able to help people in need.

I woke up to the smell of bacon cooking. Boy, it has really been a long time since I've laid in bed and could smell breakfast cooking.

I slid into my Levis and went downstairs expecting to see Nora in the kitchen.

There was Lee, apron on and flipping eggs. "How do you like your eggs, over medium as usual?"

"You bet, I answered, and my bacon crisp."

"Where's Nora?"

"Dad and Mom left out early this morning to go back over to our house; they want to see where to start on the rebuilding."

Boy, is this a fine breakfast, I thought. We sat at the table and talked about things that happened with the tornado last night.

"Where were you when the twister hit, I asked Lee?" She looked up at me while sipping her coffee. "I was in the kitchen, but I had been in bed and I woke up for some reason and had gone down to the kitchen."

"I had only been down there about ten minutes when the linoleum on the kitchen floor started raising off the floor."

"I screamed to the top of my lungs to Mom and Dad, "Tornado, Tornado."

"Their bedroom door flung open and they were in a dead run."

"Dad was still trying to pull up his pants and Mom was dragging her house coat."

"We went out the back door of the kitchen and looked off to the northwest."

"There was the funnel cloud about 200 yards away; the tail was whipping back and forth and it sounded like a freight train coming right at us."

"It was solid lightning flashing and it totally lit up the black sky."

"Luckily the storm cellar was only twenty feet from the kitchen door or we wouldn't have made it."

"Dad opened the outer door and we went down the old cement steps to the inner door, unlatched it and closed both doors behind us."

"I dropped a two by four wood beam across the inner door."

"Dad was looking for the kerosene lantern to light it." "We sat on the old spring mattress cot waiting and listening for what was coming."

"The worst part is hearing all the noise and racket and not knowing what's going on outside the cellar."

"It was over in a few minutes but the rain continued to pound against the outer cellar door."

"When it starts to rain you know the twister is past as the rain always follows the funnel."

"Dad opened the cellar doors with great anticipation and, well, you know the rest."

I reached over and lay my hand on hers. "All I can say Lee, It was really lucky that your family had that storm cellar close by or you would have never survived in that house."

"Hey, you guys up," came a loud voice from the front door?" It was Charlie and Nora. "Ya come on in, but you're late for breakfast," I kiddingly hassled Charlie. "As long as there's coffee made," Charlie answered back.

"How much of the house you think you can save or are you going to tear it down and just build you a new one, I asked?"

"Let's have that coffee first, I need a shot of caffeine really bad this morning," Charlie said, and sat down at the table, leaning back as Lee poured the coffee.

"Nora and I had a real good look at the house last night and today and we've decided to bulldoze the rest of the house down and start over fresh."

"The problem is, it'll probably take three or four months at best to build a new house from scratch."

I jumped in quick to answer, "Well, that shouldn't be a problem; you know you can stay here as long as you want. I'd be happy to help you build that new one and one other thing is that I'm looking forward to having someone in the house again."

Charlie looked at Nora to study her quiet facial expression. Nora broke out a big smile, "well, we sure do appreciate your hospitality and we're willing to accept it, but you've got to promise us that if we get in your way or you just get tired of us around, you'll just tell us outright and it won't hurt our feelings and we'll find another place to stay."

"Now you got to promise," Nora pleaded with a concerned voice. "OK Nora, I promise, I promise."

Nora, Charlie and Lee took up house keeping with me and over the next months, we were like one big happy family.

The only problem that I didn't expect was that I was really falling for Lee and when we were apart, I couldn't wait to see her again.

I get this tight gut feeling when she leaves just to go to the store.

Then at night when I look up at the stars, I can't keep from thinking of Taza.

Sometimes I think it's all a dream but I know better. It was as real as that twister that hit town and as real as the Bannerstone that hung around my neck.

The other thing, Lee is here everyday and Taza is off somewhere, maybe in another galaxy, who knows.

You know, If Taza showed up right now, I'd be back in her camp. Damn this is tough.

At least I don't have to make any life commitments at this time anyway.

I guess I'd better cool it with Lee for now anyway, because I'm afraid we're going to be in the house alone and I'll make a move on her and she might not stop me.

We've all been working hard on Charlie and Nora's new house. I spend every free minute over there pounding nails and sawing wood. The framing is finished and the roof is getting shingled.

I can't believe that Lee and I have been up on the roof nailing down shingles for three days now.

I do believe it's time we take a break tonight and go to a Drive-in movie. When I mentioned it to Lee she jumped at the idea.

At the Drive-in, they make the trucks park in the back row because the cab sets higher than a car. The people parked the row behind you can't see the movie and get really pissed.

I kind of like it like that anyway because it's really dark and more private in the back row along with all the other pickup trucks.

"Hey Lee, you want to take a shower first?" It always takes her twice as long as it does me to take a shower. She say's it takes her longer because of her hair but I think personally she just stands under the shower and lets the water run. If we have another drought this summer like we have the last few years she will be lucky to have enough water to wash up in a wash pan.

Lee replied, "Ya, I'll go first and if I use up all the hot water maybe a cold shower will do you good."

"Now what do you mean by that, I asked?" Lee answered in a giggly voice, "Well I've been noticing you have been getting a little bit horney lately."

"You've been helping me up and off the porch and squeezing me at every opportunity."

"Shoot fire Lee, I don't want you jumping off the porch and breaking a leg. We all need your help to get this house done."

Lee replied, "If you ever figure out how to build them steps at the front porch, you won't have to worry about it."

Lee closed the bedroom door about three quarters of the way. I could hear her continuing to talk about something but couldn't quite make out what she was saying. So I walked up to the door and said, "What are you mumbling about?"

As I glanced through the part open door Lee walked around the bed toward the bathroom. She was completely naked. I spun around, really embarrassed and shaking like a leaf in an autumn breeze.

I don't know what came over me but I had butterflies in my chest and stomach and my hands and arms were actually shaking.

I know what they mean when they say, "you're all shook up."

Lee had a beautiful white body. She reminded me of a white marble Greek statue I'd seen in pictures.

Ok, I got control of myself. I really felt like going in there and take her in my arms and hold her tight against me and feel her warm body against mine. I knew it wouldn't stop there and I just don't want to make that kind of commitment yet.

I reached up and touched the Bannerstone hanging against my chest. It was red hot. I guess it got excited too. I had to stop and laugh at myself.

Lee hollered, "You're next, and I did leave some hot water." Boy, I thought, if I ever needed a cold shower it was now.

Lee came out of the bedroom with a white towel wrapped around her head and a big white towel around her body. Her long white legs stuck out from the bottom of the towel like you'd see in a pin-up magazine.

I showered quickly and dressed. Lee was sitting in the front porch swing, slowly swinging back and forth.

"Ready to go", I asked as I pushed the front screen door open? "You bet I am, Lee replied in an excited voice."

She really looked sharp tonight. She was wearing a full white skirt with little green umbrellas all over it, cut low in front, "Wow."

Lee looked at me, "what is it?"

"Do I look alright?"

She had caught a gleam in my eye or a smile on my face. I answered back. "Ya, you look great."

I took her hand and we walked from the porch down the rock sidewalk to the old iron gate. As I opened it, it made that hair rising shriek. "I know, Lee said with a smile, you've got to oil that gate someday."

I opened the door to the truck and Lee got in. She gathered her skirt up in her lap so I could close the door. "Got it all in, I asked with a smirk?"

"Yes, Lee answered, just get in and let's go."

The truck started with a whirl of the engine. I dropped it into first gear and we were on our way.

Five

"**I** guess we should have checked to see what was playing at the drive-in movie", Lee commented. I answered back, "Ya, as this is the only drive-in within 40 miles, this is it."

Lee turned to me saying, "What if it's a really bad movie?"

"Hey, the popcorn will probably be good", I replied, "and you can't beat the company." Lee looked at me with raised eyebrow, "I hope you're not expecting anything else besides good company tonight?" I looked at Lee with a little grin, "Now Lee, you know what a positive attitude I have about everything and I'm just expecting a good movie."

We pulled into the drive-in movie entrance. The little square ticket booth had a lady inside with the tickets and the money box and a guy outside collecting the money and handing out tickets.

He walked up to the truck. "How many?" I looked at Lee and she looked back smiling. "I think there will be two tonight", I answered.

The older fellow spoke with a lisp; "Ya know you got to park in the back row?"

"Ya, I know, because the truck is so tall, the people in the cars can't see over it."

He leaned in the window and said, "You got it Cowboy." "Two bucks, and I ain't gonna charge you any more cause you're ugly."

He handed over two tickets and laughed loudly at his own joke. I wasn't overjoyed with his sense of humor but the way he said it was funny I'll admit.

We pulled onto the right hand road that ran around the last row of speakers and I swung the truck in close as possible to a speaker stand so the speaker could hang on the window on my side of the truck.

The ramp was steep in this row I guess because of the trucks, so I backed up to get the angle of sight just right so we could lean back in the seat and see the movie screen straight on.

"This OK," I asked Lee?" She answered excitedly, "Yes, it's perfect and I noticed on the way in, the movie tonight is, "Love me Tender", with Elvis Presley and he's the grooviest."

"The movie is going to start in about fifteen minutes," I noted as I checked my wrist watch. "How about I go down to the concession stand and wrestle us up a couple of hotdogs and cokes?" Lee replied, "That sounds great."

"I'll be right back so hold down the fort while I'm gone."

She smiled as I got out of the truck; knocking the speaker off the truck door window and watching it bite the dusty ground. I picked it up, hung it back on the window and headed for the concession stand.

I had just walked past three rows of speakers when I felt the Bannerstone getting extremely warm. I reached down the front of my shirt and touched the stone.

Taza was sending me a message. I turned to the East and looked up. My eyes caught a glimpse of what looked like a meteor or falling star going south.

I knew that I was being called by Taza and her message rang loud and clear in my mind. She would be at the box canyon tonight.

Oh boy, it looks like decision time. How am I going to pull this one off with Lee with me? I just can't leave the movie and take her home with no reason and I can't lie to her.

This is great, I thought in disgust. What to do, what to do. Well, first I'm going to the concession stand.

As I continued to walk I thought about what Taza had told me about communication via the Bannerstone. I still had my hand grasping the Bannerstone.

I concentrated my thoughts toward Taza saying, "I'll have to meet you at 12 O'clock tomorrow night in the canyon." Taza came back immediately saying, "I got your message; remember, the Bannerstone tells all when you have it activated."

I felt embarrassed because she had heard all my thoughts. The

Bannerstone cooled; it was alright to meet her tomorrow night.

I got back to the truck with the hotdogs and drinks. I handed them through the open window to Lee.

She looked me right in the eye, "what was that all about?" "What," I replied. Lee looked at me with her turned up eyebrow saying, "I saw you reaching under your shirt and grab onto that stone you wear around your neck."

"I also saw the look on your face, so what's coming off here?" Oh boy, I didn't even think about Lee seeing me. I guess I was pretty obvious.

"I'll tell you what it looked like", Lee blurted out. "It looked like you had a sudden urge to pray but you couldn't because you were in the middle of a drive-in movie theater on the way to get hotdogs."

"I want to know what's going on with you."

Thoughts were running around in my head like lightening strikes but I just stood there looking blank.

I thought I might as well tell her the truth. What? I couldn't tell her the truth, she'd think I was nuts for sure.

Lee sit glaring at me waiting for an answer. "Well, Lee spoke in a discussed tone, I'm waiting and I would appreciate the truthful version; that would be good."

I can tell she is really pissed at me by that tone of voice. "Well Lee here it is. I got this urgent call from a space ship and they want me to meet them tonight and I told them that I couldn't right now because I was busy having a date."

"Well, Lee said, that's the biggest and fattest lie I ever heard in my life, but I get it; you don't plan on telling me anything about what's going on and I'll tell you something, I am not planning on sitting next to a bigot and a liar."

"Hey", I don't even know what a bigot is; should I be happy or mad at your comment?"

Lee fired back, "A bigot is someone just like you that thinks you can't share or trust anyone else with your inner feelings."

"Okay Lee, I am sorry I was so blunt and blew my lid, but I've got a real big problem and I really need your help to solve it."

Lee gave me a questioning look. "You want me to help you solve a problem after that big story you just laid on me?"

I could tell Lee was somewhat pissed and it would take some real honesty and persistence to get the trust back.

"Lee, I want to be honest and serious about this so please cut me some slack."

"I need you to understand and it's very important to me."

"You're a very intelligent, unique, solid, Kansas born and bred girl and I need your help."

"Rolf", Lee replied softly, I do want to help, and I'm sorry for getting so uptight and I'm ready to listen if you promise to be straight with me."

"Hey, the hotdogs are getting cold and the ice is melting in the cokes and the movie is getting ready to start, so how about us getting back to this after the movie, OK?"

Lee replied with a cute little half grin, "OK Rolf, but after the movie, you've got to come clean."

I reached over and put my arm around Lee, she snuggled in close, we settled back to watch the movie.

Six

We drove along the sand road headed toward home. The Jackrabbits were cris-crossing the road in front of the truck headlights.

The Fox and Coyotes population had been on the decrease over the past seven years and the Rabbit population had exploded.

You can't find a tumble weed out here without a Jackrabbit under it. I marvel at how nature balances itself.

If something in the food chain gets out of balance, it affects everything else.

Lee rose up in the seat pointing up the road in front of us; "Hey, look at that big Jackrabbit coming straight down the road towards us."

I slammed on the brakes but the truck slid like it was on ice. The rear end of the truck slid around like it was trying to pass us. Then the truck went airborne as we went over an embankment and the truck landed with a crashing thud on its wheels.

The truck sat rocking back and forth. I looked over at Lee. Her eyes were as big as saucers.

I asked, "Are you alright?" She looked shaken as she replied, "Ya, I'm alright, at least I think so; lucky we didn't hit a fence or a tree."

"Ya, I answered, I'm going to get out and see what kind of shape we're in."

"I hope I can pull out of this ditch." I swung the door open and I could see immediately that we were not going to just drive out of this one without a tractor pulling us out. "It looks like we're going to have to take a walk in the dark tonight."

"I'll borrow a tractor tomorrow morning from old Jack Schroeder."

"I think we're only about two miles from his farm." I made my way slowly around the truck in the dark as the headlights reflected off the ravine's steep bank.

I reached the door on Lee's side and fumbled for the door handle. Suddenly Lee opened the door, smacking my hand and then me. I fell backwards; over I went into the ditch, head over heels landing flat of my back with a crashing sound of old tree branches breaking under the weight of my body.

I had landed in the bottom of the ditch where a farmer had thrown old hedge tree branches to stop the erosion and the washing out of the ditch when it rained.

I could feel the darned thorn's sticking me all over the back through my shirt. I hollered at Lee, "be careful when you step out, there's a big wash out next to the truck and I'm in the bottom of it flat of my back."

I hadn't even got the last word out of my mouth when I heard a loud shriek from Lee and she come tumbling down and rolling. "Oh man", I hollered.

Lee had landed right on top of me, kicking and a screaming. I could feel the thorns digging into my back. "Lee, Lee, whoa settle down."

"I think we're alright, but can you get off me?" Lee tried to get up. I realized she had landed butt first sitting on my chest and her shoes was kicking me on both sides of my head.

She slid forward, I could feel her legs on both sides of my face and then "Muff". I tried to holler out but she was sitting butt straight on my face.

Lee was trying to get her feet under her but the brush pile kept breaking under her weight. Her weight was smashing the back of my head down through the brush. I could feel her tight stretched panties slide back and forth over my face.

I was trying to grab on to her legs or thighs but all I could get hold of was her loose dress. She lunged forward, her butt slid off my face and over my forehead.

It slid so fast, it felt like rope burn on my face and forehead. Lee was moaning and groaning as the thorns was eating into her legs and bottom.

Finally she shouted, "Rolf," I'll never go to another movie with you as long as I live." I couldn't help it, I started laughing; I never expected to hear that statement at this particular time.

Then Lee started laughing; saying, "we really know how to have a good time together don't we." We both lay in the brush pile laughing in pitch darkness, thorns sticking us all over.

If people would have seen us, they would have thought we had escaped from an insane asylum.

"Well, let's see if we can get out of this brush pile and get back up on the road, I exclaimed as I tried to roll over on my stomach."

"Each time I try to put weight on these rotten branches they break." Lee commented back, "ya, I'm standing in brush up to my crotch and still don't have anything solid to stand on."

I finally rolled over three or four times until I could feel some strong limbs below my feet. I got to my feet after a struggle and shouted to Lee; "Stay still till I can get over to help you out."

The truck lights were shining against the bank reflecting enough light to see around a small area. I spotted an old tree limb that looked like it had been trimmed up to make a fence post. They probably left it because it was a little small and crooked.

It was just the thing I needed to get Lee out of the brush pile. I picked up the limb and made my way over towards Lee.

"Here Lee, take hold of this post and lay it across in front of you and put your weight down on it and see if you can pull yourself up."

"It'll give you something solid to work with." Lee agreed saying, "I'm really stuck tight in these darn branches." I worked the post out to her, she grabbed onto the end of it. She worked with it feverishly and I could hear the brush snapping and a cracking. Finally Lee shouted back. "Rolf, hang on to the end of the post and see if you can pull me out."

She swung the end of the post around and I made a grab at it but missed.

"Can you roll the post back towards me, I asked?"

"I can see the end of it; "I got it, hold on tight, I'm going to pull easy."

Lee shouted back, "Hold it tight, I think I can pull myself out sideways." It sounded like a bulldozer in that brush pile.

Finally, Lee shouted back, "I'm out," and she came crawling out with the help of the post. Lee struggled to her feet grabbing on to my hand like it was a life line tossed to a drowning person.

We struggled up the bank to the front of the truck headlights. We stood looking at the hundreds of scratches we had on our arms.

Lee raised her dress to expose her blood stained legs. She had scratches all the way up to her panty line. "Lee, I really feel bad about all this, so the least I can do is play doctor and fix your wounds?" Lee turned and gave me the raised eyebrow treatment, "You're really quick to want to play doctor for me when you're scratched up as bad as I am."

Lee continued," I'll tell you what; you can repair wounds below the knees and from my finger tips to my elbows and I'll volunteer to do the same for you?"

"Also, I have some alcohol at home that will fix those cuts, it's called painless alcohol." Lee laughed at her own not so funny joke.

I reached into the truck and turned off the headlights. Wow, did it get dark in a hurry. We walked down the sand road in the dark night.

If you looked almost straight up you could make out the outline of an occasional hedge tree line. One good thing out here, the roads all run north, south, east, and west in square miles so every mile you walk, you come to another crossroad. The only thing you have to be careful of on a pitch black night like tonight is that it's easy to get turned around and walk the wrong direction. Especially, when there is no moon light or stars to give you a reference.

I was right about the location where we had gone in the ditch. We had walked about two and a half miles and I could see a light burning in the Schroeder's kitchen. They only have a small single light bulb hanging from the kitchen ceiling.

"You know Lee, old man Schroeder gets up really early every morning."

"He goes to the kitchen before any one else is even thinking of being up and sits at the kitchen table and reads his Bible."

"I've been past their house at 5:00 A.M., taking the tractor to the field to plow, and I could see him sitting at the table reading his Bible."

"Yea, Lee answered, if he practiced what he read, he'd be a real saint."

"You should have heard him once when me and my two girl friends went over to their pond to swim one Sunday afternoon."

"You know that big 10 acre pond south of their cow barn; sits way back in the pasture?"

"Well, Jan Simmons, Ashley Barnes and I decided to go skinny dipping."

"It was a really hot summer Sunday afternoon and we thought that would be a great way to cool off from the heat."

"Old man Schroeder has that land posted with no trespassing signs about every thirty feet all around that land."

"He say's he hates city hunters that come out to hunt because they shoot anything that moves and they ride down his fences climbing over them."

"Well, our family has been swimming in his pond ever since I was born and he never cared."

"We would open the gate and drive back and park at the end of the pond dam and spread out a picnic lunch."

"We'd all swim and spend the whole afternoon there, and like I said, he never cared."

"Well, this particular afternoon, things were a little different."

"We three girls had walked through the field, climbed over the fence and made our way on down to the pond."

"There was a bunch of brush and trees at the end of the dam, great shade and really hid from anyone seeing you dress or undress, which ever the case."

"Well, that's where Jan, Ashley and I undressed and hung our clothes on some low growing brush and slipped into the water."

"I remember it was really cold at first, even on a hot day, but we got used to it after ducking under and swimming around awhile."

"We probably swum for about two hours or so and we decided it was time to head back home because it was a long walk back."

"We had just stepped out of the water and I started to dress when we heard a thundering of hoofs coming through the brush."

"It was old man Schroeder's buck sheep with two of his females."

"We took off running to find the nearest tree to climb."

"Thank God I had already got my panties and bra on because when I started up that tree there was no time to hesitate." "That buck sheep was right on my heels."

"Ashley and Jan had each found a tree and climbed it."

"The old buck sheep would run to one tree, then over to the next, trying to get one of us."

"He had a set of horns that rolled back over his neck and He was really a beautiful specimen of a buck sheep but he also had a bad temper."

"If he got a chance he'd butt you hard enough to knock you flying through the air."

"We'd holler back and forth tree to tree discussing the situation."

"We decided we'd wait him out and he'd get tired of running tree to tree and just leave, but no such luck."

"He decided to lie down between the three trees and rest." "Ashley had an idea."

"Her and Jan would make a lot of noise, shake the trees and holler to get the buck's attention."

"I would sneak down the tree and get behind the dam."

"Then work my way across the field to the Schroeder house and get old man Schroeder to come and get his buck sheep." "The reason I got elected to go, was I had more clothes on than anyone else."

"Well, the plan worked; when Ashley and Jan started hollering and shaking the tree, the buck jumped up and ran over to their trees and I slid down out of the tree."

"I made my way around behind the pond dam and took off to the barn and then to the house."

"I knocked on the door trying to cover myself as much as possible."

"I hoped Mrs. Schroeder would answer the door but no such luck."

"Old man Schroeder opened the door and stood frozen in the doorway."

"What are you doing, where are your clothes?"

"The old man was stuttering and stammering, I think he was more embarrassed than I was."

"I stood there on the porch trying to explain what had happened and that we needed him to come and get his buck sheep."

"All he could say was, "well, I'll be gawd damm.""

"Mrs. Schroeder had heard the commotion and popped around the old man."

"She grabbed my arm and pulled me into the kitchen and on to the bedroom."

"She grabbed a bathrobe and through it around me." She was almost tearful saying," you poor child, I've told and told Jack about that buck sheep."

"He's a mean one, especially when he's got his females around him."

"She went on to say, "That darned sheep chased me clear across the barn yard this week; I got over the board fence just in time.""

"Well, Mrs. Schroeder found me a pair of her old slacks and a shirt to slip into and then Mr. Schroeder and I walked back to the pond and he was a fussin and a grumbling the whole time."

"He just walked up to the buck sheep waved his arms and hollered, "get to the barn.""

"The old buck sheep and the females took off running."

"I went over to where all of our clothes were and started picking them off the brush branches and walked back to where Ashley and Jan were making their way down out of the trees." "They were naked as new hatched birds."

"I couldn't believe old man Schroeder never missed seeing all that he could see."

"Ashley yelled out, "Turn around you old fart.""

"The old man spun on his heels saying, "I don't want to ever see any of you back on my property again, you hear that, he shouted.""

"We all chimed in, "don't worry about us ever being back here again."

"Rolf, it's one of those experiences you don't forget anytime soon, Lee explained, and you know I'm not looking forward to knocking on his door again."

Lee continued," Especially in the middle of the night; with a boy and me looking all scratched up and my dress half torn off."

"Well Lee, it's like this, either we ask for help or we walk back to town." Lee grabbed hold of my arm tightly saying, "I'd rather walk twenty miles to town then face that old man." I could tell she was dead serious, so we kept on walking towards town.

Seven

It was starting to get daylight when we reached the city limits of town. It was strange but, walking along the road holding Lee's hand and talking about anything and everything, I could really feel a closeness to Lee and it really felt good.

Finally we came to our yard gate and up the sidewalk to the front door. Man, it was a long night, but I think it's going to be a longer day today.

No sleep last night and I'm probably going to shower and then go get a tractor and pull my truck out of the ditch. I need to get it out of that ditch soon as possible.

Everyone in town will know about my truck and be asking me a boat load of questions about what happened.

Lee hit the shower first and then I took mine. I washed off the blood from the dozens of scratches I had encountered.

I touched the Bannerstone as I rinsed the soap off my chest. It was hot. I grabbed hold of it with both hands and a thought flooded my mind.

Taza was sending me a message reminding that we need to meet tonight at the canyon, 12:00 midnight. I acknowledged I would meet her there. The Bannerstone turned cold instantaneously.

I dressed quickly and went down stairs to the kitchen. Lee was standing beside the kitchen table with an odd look on her face.

"Hey", I asked, what's the matter with you?" Lee looked me straight in the eye. "OK, how did you pull this one off, she blurted out."

"What are you talking about?" She pointed out the window. There sat my truck in the yard. Low and behold, someone had went and got my truck out of the ditch and parked it beside the garage.

"Well, I don't know how it got there but I'm sure glad it's there." Lee came back with a quick response. "Yea, I'll bet you called a wrecker truck while I was in the shower and figured you'd pull a joke on me, making me think we had to walk someplace to get a tractor."

I turned Lee around and laid my hands on her shoulders. "Lee, I honestly don't know how the truck got there; I didn't call anyone and it just so happens, I have the only ignition key right here in my hand."

Lee and I walked out on the back porch and down the steps to the stone footpath that led to the garage. I couldn't help from thinking that Taza might have something to do with this but, no, that's probably far out thinking.

I walked around the truck looking for tire marks where a wrecker might have towed it but no visible tire marks, even in the sand. Now I was getting afraid that Taza did have something to do with this and I'd never be able to explain this one.

"Hey Rolf," a voice came from behind me. I turned around quickly. It was old man Jack Schroeder. "I see you found your truck," as he chuckled loudly. "It looks like they need to widen these roads so you young people can keepum between the ditches."

"When my wife Julie and I drove out the road this morning, we spotted it setting in the ditch."

"Figured you'd need it out so we drove back to the house and I picked up my flat bed truck, loaded her up and hauled it over."

I reached out and shook Jack's big old callused hand saying," Man do I ever appreciate it; I wasn't sure how I was going to get it out of the ditch."

I couldn't help from asking Jack how he got the truck unloaded without leaving a tire mark. When I asked him about it, he looked at me with a big question mark on his face. He stood looking around the ground, searching for the tire tracks he'd made in the sand. "Well I'll be darned," Jack blurted out, rubbing his chin, "I don't know what happened to them because I left plenty of tracks all over the place."

"Maybe the wind blew the tracks out, Hell, I don't know." "Yea, I echoed in, I'll bet that's what happened, I'll bet the wind blew some of that loose sand and dirt over them and covered them over." Neither Jack nor I bought the explanation but neither of us had a better thought.

While Jack and I were discussing the lack of tracks, Lee had cornered Julie and they were both talking excited about something.

Jack and I strolled over to see what the excitement was. Julie was telling Lee that she had seen a flying saucer late last night, and she had tried to keep it to herself and not tell anyone but she just couldn't keep quiet about it.

She just had to tell the first person besides Jack what she had seen. "I know no one is going to believe me because I don't know whether I believe it myself, but I seen it and I know I seen it."

"Last night the dogs were barking outside really excited and I knew something was around because old Justice, you know, our old blind dog, well she never lies and she is sensitive to things the other dogs aren't even aware of."

"Well, she was barking up a storm so I got up from bed and pulled the window shade back."

"There it was; sitting on the ground in the pasture beside the barn, blue hazy lights flashing on and off."

"It had a rounded nose around the outside, not like one of those cartoon drawings where they have a sharp edge."

"It made no distinct noise, more like a humming sound."

"I hollered to Jack, "look what's in the pasture!""

"Jack rolled over to see what I was talking about."

"Come here and look at this," I shouted hysterically. "I turned back to look out the window just catching a glimpse of it shooting off into the sky."

"I have never seen anything move so fast in all my life." "By the time Jack got to the window it was gone." "Naturally, he didn't believe a word I said and tried to convince me that I had a bad dream or nightmare."

"Well, I'm here to tell you, I seen what I seen and nobody is telling me different." Hearing Julie's story, I walked up and put my arm around her and spoke softly in her ear. "I know you seen a flying object because I have seen the same thing."

Julie pulled away from me saying," Are you teasing me Rolf or are you being serious?"

"Julie", I said, "I'm being totally honest with you; I saw the same thing you just described." Julie started asking me a barrage of questions and I didn't want to say any more about it, I thought I'd already said too much. "I really would like to talk about it later Julie, if that's alright?" Julie looked a little disappointed but nodded her head in approval saying,"OK Rolf, but I'd like to hear the particulars when and where you saw this thing."

"I promise Julie, I'll tell you everything."

I thought to myself, I really don't know how I'm going to explain any of this.

I turned back to Jack," come on in the house for some breakfast, Lee and I were just getting ready to cook up some bacon and eggs."

Jack looked over at Julie as if to get her approval. Julie shot back;"now Rolf, have you ever seen a time when Jack Schroeder would turn down food?" Joking I said," A working man has got to keep up his strength." Julie answered back quickly; "If that was true, Jack would be the strongest man in the country."

Lee started for the house with Julie; that means Jack and I could sit on the porch and talk till breakfast was ready.

Charlie and Nora were up and Nora had made coffee. It's great having Charlie, Nora and Lee here; they really feel like family. Nora hollered through the screen door," You all want some coffee?" I answered quickly, "You bet we do."

Jack and I sat on the front porch steps drinking coffee and discussing the wheat crop and weather. Charlie came out and sat down on the porch step with us. Jack said," Charlie, how are you making out with your new house?"

"Got it under roof," Charlie exclaimed. "Rolf has been steady helping and even Lee was putting down shingles this week".

Lee popped out through the screen door saying,"Breakfast is ready and you better be hungry."

"Don't worry Lee," Charlie said in a low laid back voice, "I think we got the right crew to handle that job." We all sat down to a table full of food and pigged out. I don't think Jack had eaten for a week the way he put away the biscuits, gravy, eggs and bacon.

"Boy, what a breakfast," Jack committed as he slid his chair back from the kitchen table. "Maybe you ought to run in the ditch more often Rolf so I can end up over here for breakfast."

"Jack laughed holding his over stuffed stomach. We sat around the table and talked while we sipped even more coffee. We were all about to float away from drinking so much coffee.

Jack was commenting that he needed to go to Uniontown to get a part for his hay baler. He was saying how he didn't really want to drive to Uniontown but he needed to get his baler fixed so he could bale hay tomorrow.

I got the message loud and clear. Jack was hinting for a volunteer to drive over to Uniontown to pick up those baler parts. Due to the fact he pulled my truck out of the ditch and delivered it to my house, I felt obligated to go.

"Jack," I said, as I looked over my shoulder at Lee, "Lee and I would be more that happy to get them parts for you and besides, I've got some business to take care of over there." Jack beamed with joy. "I would really appreciate it."

"I'd rather be beat with a whip then drive all the way over to Uniontown."

Lee had a big smile on her face so I knew she approved. "Just let me know what you want us to pickup and we'll head over there this morning." I looked over at Lee; "Right Lee?" She answered back quickly, "Just try to get away without me and besides, I know more about a hay baler than you do."

Charlie chimed in,"Ya, She's even a better mechanic then she is a cook."

"I remember one time she baked her first pie, you couldn't cut the crust with a knife or a sharp saw."

"I always said, I wished she could remember how she made that crust, because you could make shoe soles out of it and they'd never wear out." Lee fired back, "Ya, but you sure don't complain about my pies now, or don't you want me to make anymore?"

"Whoa now," Charlie shot back, "You make the best darn pies I ever ate." I broke in quickly because I knew Charlie had just put his foot in his mouth. "Now Charlie, you know Nora ain't going to take kindly to that statement about who makes the best pies so Lee and I are heading out for Uniontown before you're stuck with baking the pies; if you ever want another one." Jack leaned back in his chair laughing like he'd never heard anything so funny. I don't think any of us could picture Charlie in an apron trying to make a pie.

Lee and I got into the truck, drove out the lane and headed for Uniontown. "Lee," I said, there's a short cut to Uniontown but it's a sand road and it goes over Uniontown hill."

"Have you ever been that way?" Lee answered back, "No but I'm game if you are." I swung off the highway onto the sand and dirt road.

We drove along with the dust boiling up in the truck. Lee was a hardened farm girl and didn't even notice the dust. Lee slid over next to me and I put my arm around her shoulder.

We had drove about an hour when we saw Uniontown hill in front of us. They used to have to back the old Model T Fords up the hill backwards because they didn't have fuel pumps on those old engines, only gravity feed. The hill was so steep, all the gas ran to the back of the tank and the motor would starve for gas and quit running.

I shifted into second gear and pushed the accelerator to the floor. The old Ford truck was crying before we got half way up the hill. I reached for the gear shift to put it into 1st gear. Lee had her legs clutched around the gear shift knob and all I could feel was legs. "If you don't want to walk you better let me shift into low gear." Lee laughed as she moved her legs apart so I could shift into low.

We were slowing to a crawl speed. "Lee", I think we're going to have to get out and push," I jokingly commented. Lee started to open the door. I shouted, "No, I was only kidding, we'll make it, slow but sure."

Lee looked at me with a discussed look saying, "If someone had to push, I knew it would be me?" I grinned, speaking in a teasing voice, "Well you know, it being my truck and all, you know I'd have to stay behind the wheel and steer."

Lee spun around, both knees in the seat and grabbed me around the neck and started biting my ear lobe. I was hollering like a trapped rabbit. "Lee", I shouted,"Stop, I've got to drive!" She was having fun and she had me right where she wanted me and I couldn't do a darn thing about it but holler.

She finally let go my ear and let loose the strangle hold she had around my neck and rolled back against the door laughing. Her full skirt had slid up over her knees and her chin was resting on them;

her arms wrapped around her legs pulling them tight to her. Her long white legs stood out against the background of white panties.

"Lee", you've got to behave yourself or we'll never get to Uniontown today." This woman was really getting to me. I wanted to be with her all the darn time but I never knew what to expect next. Best of all, she was really fun to be with.

The truck finally reached the crest of Uniontown hill. Now, we've got to start down the other side. I kept it in low gear so I could to save on the brakes as they really got hot going down the steep hill.

The road was straight down like the other side was straight up. Why anyone would build a road over the mountain instead of around it had to be lacking something up stairs. Knowing Surveyors and Engineers, they love to keep these neat little square miles of highway straight as a string.

The truck picked up speed as we made our decent down. The engine was starting to scream and I was ridding the brakes hard. I could smell the brake linings start to smoke. I finally pushed the brake pedal down hard and pulled to the shoulder of the road.

"I've got to let these brakes cool or they will get so hot they will fade out and then it's wide open to the bottom of the hill."

We sat in the truck for a few minutes but the smoke was coming up in the truck and boy did it stink. I turned to Lee,"Let's get out of here before we both smell like burnt brake shoes." We both flung open the doors and got out in haste. I rested my foot on the running board and leaned back against the truck cab. The weather was starting to get hot for this early in the morning. As I leaned forward I felt a hot spot against my chest. The Bannerstone was heating up. Taza wanted to communicate. I reached my hand inside my shirt and grabbed hold of the stone. It was HOT. I cleared my thoughts. I knew the message was from Taza. "Important", must see you." It must be really important because all the other times she needed to see me it's always been,"I'd like to see you."

Lee walked around the front of the truck. She never misses catching me with an obvious look on my face. "Lee blurted out," what's wrong with you?"

I jerked my foot off the running board and straightened up still clutching the Bannerstone in my hand. "Come here Lee," I said with a strong commanding voice. Lee looked at me with astonishment. She rarely ever heard me speak in that tone of voice. "Sure", Lee answered.

"Get a hold of this Bannerstone and tell me what you feel." Lee reached out and touched the black stone. "I can't believe it's so hot."

"Just hang on to it for a few minutes." Lee wrapped her hand around the stone firmly. I could see her eyes lighting up. "Wow," she exclaimed," this is awesome."

"I can hear words like someone is talking to me but it's talking to my mind not my ears." Lee's eyes were big as saucers and she was almost gasping to get the words out."

"It's a woman's voice and she called me by my name and that she is pleased to meet me at last!" Lee had a totally puzzled look on her face. She was staring a hole right through me. I reached up putting my hand over Lee's as she held the Bannerstone. We could both mentally hear Taza asking that we meet with them and she would explain the details of this important problem and confirm date and time of the meeting.

Taza closed by telling Lee that I would fill in the necessary details surrounding the Bannerstone. The stone started cooling off immediately.

"Ok Rolf, let's hear the details," Lee blurted out with her mouth twitched to one side. "It's a long story Lee."

We both sat down on the tail gate of the pickup and I started at the beginning, explaining my first encounter with Taza and her father and later how her father had given me the Bannerstone.

We sat and talked for over an hour. Lee listened not to miss a word. I also talked to her about the night of the tornado and the little Govia girl and all the meetings I had with Taza including a detailed description of the space craft.

Lee sat soberly looking at me. "I wouldn't believe any of this, even if you told me it was true, if I hadn't heard it for myself."

Without blinking an eye, Lee said, "How do you suppose they do that?"

"Ya, I know," I replied. "I think they are a few hundred or thousand years ahead of us in technology."

"Ya, Lee said, Taza told me I was not to ask any questions of her or disclose to anyone concerning the encounter."

"Being a woman herself, she sure knows how to put a hurting on another woman; can't tell something like this to anybody!" Lee grinned as she thought about what she had just said.

Well, this is a huge relief to me because I didn't have a clue as to how I was ever going to explain this to Lee and I think Taza knew it, and bailed me out. I know now why she's driving a space vehicle and I'm driving a old Ford truck.

Lee and I got back in the truck. The brakes had cooled and we were ready to go on to Uniontown to get those parts for Jack. Lee continued to talk about the bannerstone and the fact that she was actually going to meet someone from another planet.

She was just about to bust with enthusiasm. I reminded her that she knew she couldn't say anything to anyone no matter what. Lee shook her head yes, but that little twitch in the corner of her mouth, leaves me with the impression that it is going to be one of the hardest things she has ever had to do.

Lee turned to me with a very serious look, "you know, I will never be the same person I was, because once being exposed to something of this magnitude, it's just not possible to think like you did before about anything."

"Hey Lee, cool it down, you're already starting to talk like Taza." I continued, "Taza told me about the same thing, and I told her I understand and will handle it and I expect you to do the same, Ok?" Lee shrugged her shoulders as if to say, I guess so.

Eight

We pulled up front of the Farm implement dealership. There was a big "John Deere" sign swinging back and forth like it was trying to cope with the everyday blowing Kansas wind. The sign hung from the overhang of the store front that also shaded the sidewalk.

A line of old oak chairs were sitting in front of the store window and every one of them had an old farmer sitting in them. Some were playing checkers, others were playing cards. "What are you playing?" I asked as we walked up to the stores front door. "Euchre," what else," was the response from one of the old farmers. He didn't even look up to see who was talking to. He was deeply absorbed in playing cards.

Lee and I went inside the store. There was everything you could think of hanging on the walls. Old horse collars, milk buckets, harness, tractor umbrellas and about anything you could hang on a wall.

There was a narrow path about a foot wide that wound its way through the store. Near the middle of the store was a large round open area where an old black pot bellied wood stove sat.

That's where all the farmers migrate from the front porch when the weather got cold or rainy.

My Dad used to bring me in here when I was really young. This place brings back a lot of good old memories.

Milo Boles, the owner, had a collection of toy tractors and machinery that always caught my eye and one year Dad bought me a John Deere tractor for Christmas and I still have it at home sitting on the fire place mantle.

I used to make roads in the dirt in the back yard and push that tractor around those roads, even built little wood stick bridges. Mom was always hollering because I wore the knees out of my pants crawling around playing with that tractor.

Lee strolled around the narrow aisle's and wondering all the way to the back of the store where Milo had his tack area.

He had Saddles, Bridles, and just about anything that would fit on a horse including western wear for the rider.

Lee had her head down in an old wooden barrel rummaging through some old clothes. She turned to me holding up a pair of old leather chaps saying, "You don't see many of these anymore do you?"

"Only in the old western movies," I commented. "You know you'd look good in a pair of those and maybe a pair of spurs to go on those cowgirl boots of yours." Lee continued to search through the barrels and wooden boxes.

"Now this is what I really need," holding up an old leather cowgirl riding shirt. Lee was really giving this skirt the once over.

She slid her hand into the front side pocket and pulled out an old brown piece of paper. Lee unfolded it carefully and studied the paper intently. She motioned for me to come see what she had found.

I was more interested in the hand guns Milo had in the case and didn't hurry see to what she had found.

Before I could move Lee came over excited saying, "Look at this, isn't this a map of the old Oxhide Trail?"

"Here's the box canyon and here's Doc Watson's ranch and the wagon road heading west?" Lee got my attention in a hurry.

"That's where we are meeting Taza tonight, Lee said."

"Let me see that." I reached over to share the map with Lee. "Darned if it aint," I exclaimed.

The map was definitely old and had started splitting where it was folded. It had writing on the bottom half of the map but the letters had numbers between each one and didn't make any word. It didn't make any sense; unless it was written in some kind of code.

The first line started off with B3 C7 C6G and continued with groups of letters and numbers mixed. "Don't make any sense to me," Lee exclaimed. I folded up the paper carefully and stuck it in Lee's dress pocket. "Lee, don't say anything about this paper." Lee nodded saying, "I'm going to ask Milo how much he wants for this skirt and maybe he knows where he got it?"

Lee walked to the front of the store and leaned over the counter beside the cash register and hollered, "Hey Mr. Boles."

A wood door with the smoked up glass swung open from behind the counter and old man Milo Boles came slowly moving through the doorway.

"What'ca need girl?" Milo squinted one eye, wiping his mouth with one hand.

Lee answered, "Hey, we didn't mean to get you away from the table."

"We'll wait to you finish lunch; we're not in that big a hurry."

"No, no," Milo came back, "customer's first, feed bag second."

"What can I do for you?"

"Well we need some parts for a hay baler; here's a list of part numbers." Lee handed Milo the list. Milo glanced over the list. "Yep, this must be for Jack Schroeder's antique baler."

"Ain't no body else got one of these still running."

"When the hell is Jack gonna break down and invest in some new equipment?"

"Although I'm not complaining, Jack sure does keep my spare parts business in the black."

Milo went down through the aisles picking up parts here and there and come back with an arm load. I looked at the number of parts and I remembered the few part numbers there was on the paper.

"Milo, I asked, "there are more parts here than was on Jack's list?"

"Ya, I know", Milo answered, "take these with you because I know he'll need most of them, but what he don't need, bring them back next time you're around here."

Lee couldn't hold it any longer. "How much do you want for this old ridding skirt?"

Milo looked up over his glasses. "Where'd you find that?" Lee answered, "Oh, it was back in the tack stuff, back in the far corner in some wooden boxes." Milo reached over and felt the leather skirt. "That skirt is probably so rotten it'd fall apart the first time you wore it."

Lee answered back quickly,"I only want it for a pattern to make a new one; it's a hobby of mine, making old western clothes."

"Oh", Milo slowly acknowledged, nodding his head. "How about five dollars?"

Lee looked him right in the eye. "It isn't worth more than three dollars and you ought to be paying me for hauling it off."

Milo cracked a little smile. He liked to dicker price over something like that more than eating when he was hungry. "You and Rolf are getting some expensive hay baler parts so I'm going to sell that original Western garment for say, four dollars." Lee shot back," three fifty and not a cent more." Milo rubbed his chin for a minute. "Well", due to the fact that you are a good loyal, longtime customer of mine I guess I can see my way clear to take that."

"Deal", Lee cried out. You could hear her all over the store and I thought she was going to jump over the counter and hug old Milo's neck. "By the way Milo, where did you get that skirt, I asked?"

Milo leaned back, scratched his head. "Lee, you got that out of those old wooden box crates back in the tack room?" "If I remember right, I traded a saddle for some old harness, couple of old shotguns, and a bunch of old wooded crates with some ridding gear in them."

"Now that was about thirty years ago, give or take a couple."

Lee asked, "Do you remember who you got them from?"

"Oh yes, Milo exclaimed, "It was the Watson boys, you know the Doc Watson bunch."

"They were the rowdiest boy's in the country."

"I felt like calling the Sheriff ever time I seen them come into town."

"Them boy's would come into my store and wanted everything they laid their eyes on and old Doc Watson would usually buy it for them."

"Couldn't complain about the business and the money was always cash on the barrel head."

"Those five boys always got in a fight among them selves before they left the store and I usually had to throw them out."

"Old Doc would just laugh like it was amusing to him."

"No, they came in one day with a wagon load of stuff they got out of an old line shack that was falling in and they wanted to trade the stuff for a saddle."

"I remember I really didn't want the stuff but they were such good customers; I went ahead and traded with them."

"Did you know they buy all their farm equipment from me?" Lee had been locked into every word Milo was saying but when he mentioned farm equipment, she picked up the list off the counter and started to check off the items Milo had assembled.

Milo prided himself for knowing where everything in the store was at. You could ask him for anything you needed for the farm and he could walk over and pick it up and he knew the price of it.

I really think he priced things off the top of his head figuring how much he could get you to pay for it because if you started to lay something back down after he priced it, he immediately would ask you how much you'd be willing to pay for it.

He loved to haggle or negotiate as he referred to it.

Milo loaded all the parts in a big cardboard box and pushed the box across the counter. Lee leaned over the counter saying, "How much are these baler parts?" Milo looked over his glasses squinting down at Lee. "Don't bother yourself girl with such things; I'll call Jack and let him know what parts I'm sending and how much he's spending." Milo smiled and chuckled at his joke he just cracked.

We left the store with the big cardboard box of parts and Lee with her old leather skirt folded tightly under her arm. When we got into the truck I ask Lee,"I didn't know you had a hobby of reproducing old western clothes?" Lee looked at me sheepishly," well, I really don't, that was the first thing that popped into my mind as to why I would want to buy an old rotten leather skirt."

"Pretty quick thinking Lee, I would have never thought of something like that."

"I was sure you'd come up with something besides telling Boles you found a map in the pocket and wanted him to translate it for you." Lee looked at me with astonishment. "Sometimes Rolf, you can be a real pain in the butt." I looked back at Lee. "Ya, I know, that's why you're so fond of me." Lee came back quickly, "and what makes you think I'm in the least fond of you?" I answered, "we won't go into that now, but maybe when we are not driving down a dusty road at fifty miles an hour."

We decided not to take the Uniontown hill road back home, but to take the longer route which was about ten miles further and a really flat non-exciting road.

We talked about the map and what it might mean. Lee's imagination was running wild. I finally convinced her to put the map away till we got home so we could both look at it and not have to try and drive and look at the map at the same time.

We pulled into the yard. Nora stepped out on the back porch holding her hand up shading her eyes from the sun. We got out of the truck and walked around the garage to where Nora was already starting to tell us something and neither one of us was could hear what she was saying.

"Lee squalled out; I can't hear what you are saying." We could both see the troubled expression on Nora's face. "Milo Boles called for you on the telephone Lee, just five minutes ago and he said he had something to tell you and that you should call him back soon as possible."

Lee hurried into the living room and picked up the receiver and cranked one round on the wall phone to get the operator. I could hear Lee ask the operator to ring Milo Boles Equipment Co. in Uniontown. Lee waited on the phone impatiently. Finally I heard her talking with Milo.

I was thinking to myself; I hope he didn't give her the wrong hay baler parts. Lee hung up the phone and turned to me.

"Well, what did he have to say, I asked?"

"You know", Lee started, "Milo said that we had no more than left his store when Bill Watson came into the store."

"He told Bill that he'd just sold some of that old line shack stuff he'd bought from him years ago when he was just a young boy and that he had traded him a saddle for it."

"Bill remembered the whole thing."

"Well, it seems Bill confessed, he didn't get that stuff from an old line shack but they got it from an old Indian woman that lived on their land along the creek next to the box canyon, in a run down cabin."

"She wouldn't pay her rent so the boys took some stuff to make up for what she owed."

"Bill told Milo that he would never forget that day because he never had been cursed out so furious in all his life."

"That old Indian woman called him everything she'd ever heard that was bad."

"Milo thought we'd be interested because that old leather skirt I bought was a real hand made Indian skirt."

Lee said, "I thanked him for calling and I told him I would let everyone know that I had bought the original skirt pattern from Milo's store in Uniontown." Old Milo never misses a trick to advertise his store so I'll bet he was glad to hear that.

I turned to Lee saying," I'll get the Baler parts out of the truck." She was already showing the leather skirt to Nora and didn't hear a word I'd said.

I heard the screech of the front yard gate open. Jack and Julie were coming up the sidewalk towards the house. "Hey you two", I yelled out, "we've got something to show you; come on in the house."

Charlie, Nora and Lee were all sitting around the living room table with the leather skirt in front of them talking about how it was stitched together. Jack and Julie sat down at the table.

Jack looked around the table saying,"What have you got there?" I answered back, "Did you ever know of an old Indian woman living in a run down cabin back of Doc Watson's Ranch near a box canyon?" Jack's head jerked up quickly, "You bet I do," he answered with an excitement in his voice. "That was Morning Dove; she was a full blood Cherokee Indian Princess; daughter of Chief Junalaska."

"My Mom and Dad knew all about her." Jack's expression changed to the serious. "Why are you asking about her?"

"Well Jack, it's a long story but I'd like to start by showing you this old leather Indian skirt that Lee bought in Milo's Boles store." Jack picked up the leather skirt and examined it closely. "I bet you got some of Morning Doves clothes."

Lee looked up astonished. "Do you really think so?" Jack answered, "Yep, it's got to be; so you tell me you got these at Milo's store?"

That was all the prompting that Lee needed. Lee was dying to tell the whole story, she couldn't hold back any longer. She went into great detail telling about how she found the skirt and that she got Milo down on price. Also about Bill Watson coming into Milo's store just after we left and what he had told Milo how they had acquired the skirt.

I was especially proud of her because she never mentioned the map she found in the pocket. I knew that she truly wanted us to check this out on our own.

After Lee finished telling what she knew about the skirt, she asked Jack about Morning Dove. Jack started out clearing his voice as if he was ready to give a speech.

"Well, this was my Mom and Dad's favorite story when I was growing up."

"They must have told it to us kids a thousand times."

"It all started when a bunch of settlers discovered gold in the northern part of Georgia".

"The Government figured they needed that gold to finance a war but the biggest problem was that the land belonged to the Cherokee Indians."

"The land was part of the Great Cherokee Nation Reservation."

"Well the Government just moved the army in to round up all the Cherokees and move them out west to the Oklahoma territory Reservation."

"They got every man, woman, and child they could find and the ones that went off in the mountains to hide, they put a bounty on their heads, dead or alive."

"They took everyone they could find and marched them on foot all the way to Oklahoma."

"Yep", it's something that makes you not proud of things our Government officials have done."

"Many of the people died on that march, and were buried along the trail; most from starvation and bad water."

"Well, about a month before all this moving of the Indians started, a Senator, which was a friend of the Cherokees Chief Junalaska, was in a meeting at the White House with the President."

"The President told him what they were planning to do, so the Senator went to see Junalaska and told him the plan." "Well Junalaska gathered up all the gold that everyone wore, including bracelets, buttons, necklaces and all the things like cups and pans and such."

"These were items they had made from the gold they had mined out of the tribal cave over many, many years."

"He took all the gold articles and hid them somewhere in the Blue Ridge Mountains of North Carolina."

Bannerstone 59

"There were only five Indians who knew where it was buried; Junalaska, his wife, and three Indian Braves."

"Well, Junalaska's wife was pregnant and when they started rounding up all the Cherokees, she went into labor and gave birth to a baby girl."

"The morning she was born, a white Mourning Dove sat in a tree by their lodge and cooed for hours; so they named the baby girl, Morning Dove."

"Well, the walk to Oklahoma was a brutal trip. It was a forced march and many of the Cherokees died on the trail."

"Somehow Morning Dove and her mother got separated from the group."

"Some say she slipped off one night with the baby during a heavy rain storm and others say she fell sick with the fever and they left her and the baby along the trail."

"Anyway, the Railroad Company was building the first railroad from St. Louis to Kansas City and then on through the Oklahoma Territory."

"Well, Laura and John Beggs, that's Rolf's Great Grandpappy and Grandma, they were working for the railroad."

"Laura was a tent cook and John was a foreman laying track."

"Well, they had gone into Pittsburg Kansas to pick up supplies and they run on to Morning Dove and her Mother down by Flat rock creek."

"They somehow convinced the Mother to go back with them to the railroad camp because they were having trouble with the Indians hanging around the camp wanting food and anything else they could get their hands on."

"John thought this might be an answer to his Indian problems as the wife of Junaluska carried a lot of weight and authority and respect among the Indian Tribes, and she spoke real good English to boot."

"They stayed with John and Laura through the year into the next."

"Along about spring, three Cherokees showed up at Laura's cook tent."

"They were rubbing their bellies in a big circle which meant they were hungry and wanted food."

"Laura took them around behind the tent and fed them."

"Well, Morning Dove and her mother showed up after they had eaten and they started talking in Cherokee but Laura could understand enough to know they wanted the Mother and Morning Dove to go with them."

"Sure enough when John and Laura got out bed the next morning, the Mother and baby were gone, but on the table, next to the bed, she left a little wooden box that was lined with red velvet and had little sea shells sewn to the velvet."

"In the box was five pieces of shiny and burnt rock."

"It looked like gold and was heavy but it was burnt like it came from a meteorite." Rolf jumped to his feet, "I've got those five pieces of rock in my room."

"Dad and Mom said it belonged to my Great Grandfather and Grand Mother Beggs."

"It has to be the same rocks." By this time the excitement had grown to the explosion point. "Go on Jack, what happened next, Lee asked?" Jack reared back in his chair saying,"Well, this is where the story gets interesting." "The story goes, the mother and Morning Dove and them three braves sneaked back to the North Carolina Blue Ridge Mountains to get the tribal gold they had hid before they were all rounded up and marched to Oklahoma."

"They say the reason they hadn't went back sooner to get the gold was, Government troops had been keeping close check on them at the reservation."

"After a year or so they figured the Indians were pretty settled in and weren't going any place."

"That's when the Braves figured they could slip off and no one would be the wiser."

"When the Mother, Morning Dove and the three braves got to North Carolina Mountains, a huge snow blizzard hit that first night but they were lucky enough to stay in a barn of a farmer."

"The farmer, his wife and kids, fed them and they slept in the hay loft in the barn as the blizzard continued on for three days."

"When the storm finally blew over, they found out the snow was so deep they couldn't leave and they ended up staying about two weeks in that barn."

"The Braves would go out during the day to try to find the place where the gold was hid but the snow was so deep they couldn't find it."

"The story goes that they had originally marked the place with three tomahawks stuck in trees pointing to a hidden cave where seven springs started out of the side of the mountain."

"They found the tomahawks and the springs but the snow was so deep they couldn't find the cave."

"Time was running out for the braves."

"They had to check in and be accounted for around the first of each month back at the reservation."

"If they didn't check in, they automatically put a bounty of two hundred dollars on their heads, dead or alive."

"There were always plenty of bounty hunters around just waiting for someone to be missing and they usually brought them back to the reservation dead."

"Well, the braves left the Mother and Morning Dove out there in the Blue Ridge Mountains and returned to the Oklahoma Territory Reservation."

"The Mother and Baby had somehow contacted some of the Cherokees that had hid out in the mountains during the roundup."

"They lived in the deep forest between the Blue Ridge and the Appalachian mountains and that was a place where if a white man ever went in there, they never came out."

"Anyway, when late summer rolled around, the Mother and Morning Dove showed up over next to the Watson ranch."

"Old Doc Watson's Mom and Dad either sold her the land or rented it to her so she could build her a cabin down on the creek."

"There was always braves showing up and staying around helping her build the cabin and work the little farm land next to the creek."

"They took up camping in the box canyon and no white man would go back there because rumor had it that it was sacred Indian burial ground."

"They would kill any white man that came into the canyon, so everyone just kind of left them alone, including the Watson's."

"Over the years, gold bracelets and nuggets would show up to trade for supplies."

"No one ever knew where the Gold came from; most thought it probably came out of Colorado or Mexico."

"There were also rumors that a few braves would go back to North Carolina every year and come back with pack mules loaded down."

"Most figured they were trading for supplies with their Cherokee brothers."

"After a few years, they stopped the trips and eventually the Indians all left the box canyon and they all went west except for the mother and Morning Dove."

"They lived in that old cabin by the creek the rest of their lives."

"Both of them passed away many years ago, both buried on that hill north of the creek in them big two mounds of earth."

Jack leaned back in his chair. "Well, that's about all I know about that situation," and grinned like a possum eating persimmons. I got the impression Jack loved that story and I think it is a heck of a story and more truth than fiction.

Nine

"Hey Lee," I asked, "Let's go out to the old Watson's ranch and see if that old cabin is still there."

"Plenty of daylight left and after that, maybe we can take in a movie?" Lee answered, "Great, give me time to change clothes and wash the dust off my face and I'll be ready."

Jack and I walked out to the truck to get the baler parts.

Fifteen minutes later, Lee came out looking good and ready to go. Jack gave us a big wave as we drove out of the lane and headed out toward the box canyon.

Lee had slid across the seat and up tight against me and I wrapped my arm around her shoulders and squeezed her lightly. We talked about all the things Jack had said and what Milo had told us.

We pulled off the main road that led to Doc Watson's ranch and onto the dirt road that led back to the box canyon. Lee was fanning her hand and waving her arm to keep the dust away from her face as the dust came rolling in the truck.

"This is the dustiest road in Ellsworth county," Lee exclaimed. "I guess they'll never put new sand on these old side roads in our lifetime?"

"Ya, I answered, it would take away their personality." Lee came back sarcastically, "Roads don't have personalities, they have unique characteristics and features."

"Ya, like I said; personality." We looked at each other and smiled.

We finally reached the box canyon entrance. I leaned over to Lee saying," it has always amazed me, that out here in the middle of the prairie, there's a canyon this big and a spring this clear that flows year round."

"It's a fact that it gets so dry in the summer and we don't get rain for weeks at a time, it still doesn't affect the flow of the spring."

"Rolf, don't you suppose because it's coming out of this big sandstone wall here in the back of the canyon, that it's coming from way underground and surface water doesn't affect it?"

"You got a good point Lee; that's probably why it's always so darn cold to drink."

We parked the truck and got out. Lee reached into her pocket and took out the old brown paper map and unfolded it carefully so not to tear it. We walked up next to the rounded front fender and leaned back against the hood.

Lee spread the map out on the hood and was turning it around and around to try to match the landmarks on the map to the surrounding terrain.

"There's a big rock over to the left side of the canyon that matches the map," Lee exclaimed in an excited voice.

"There's where the old cabin and the corral should be," pointing to the right. "Come on Rolf; let's find the old cabin or what's left of it."

We walked around the clumps of tumble weed while we made our way toward the northeast canyon wall. According to the map, the main creek bed was supposed to be running through that low spot, but the creek is actually another three hundred yards east.

"I'll bet the creek used to run right through here," I commented. "What do you think Lee?" Lee was studying the map with intensity.

The frown on her face suddenly changed to a smile. "I'll bet so too Rolf and that'll put the cabin near the back of the canyon on the east side."

We continued moving around the rocks that stood up like tall totem poles and then made our way through the sage brush and thistles and sure enough, nestled down behind two overhanging rocks, stood the old cabin.

It didn't look like it was in that bad of condition. I expected it to be a lot worse. I had visualized it was constructed from logs, but it was made of sandstone.

The roof looked rotted and the front door was hanging. Vines had taken over the roof and hid the cabin really well.

We grabbed hold of the hanging wooden door, which was standing half open, and pulled the door open. The walls and floor were all sandstone and the roof was wooden poles covered with shingles.

Each stone in the sandstone walls was about eight feet long and about a foot square. Each large stone was precision stacked and fit together without a crack between them.

The window openings in the sandstone walls were about a foot above the outside ground level and the inside floor about three feet below ground level.

It was probably built this way to be warm in the winter and cool in the summer.

Lee and I were amazed of the good condition the sandstone floors and walls were after years of being abandoned and exposed to the weather.

Lee turned and said," Rolf, Let's look at that map again." Lee pulled the map from her pocket and we both studied the faint lines and symbols on the old map.

"Lee", you know this map shows another door in the cabin."

"To be exact, the back wall should have a door right here."

I pointed to the smooth sandstone wall. "Lee, something just doesn't add up."

"Why draw a door in the cabin that doesn't exist?" Lee answered slowly as if she was trying to figure it out as she spoke. "Well maybe there was a door there when the cabin was built and then it was sealed up for some reason."

I ran my hands along the smooth sandstone wall trying to detect a crack or a sigh where a door had been. Sure enough, a crack where the sandstone had chipped and broken off.

I pulled out my pocket knife and started digging around the chipped off area.

The crack had been skillfully sealed with sandstone and the more I dug the more I could start to make out a sealed doorway.

Lee and I dug around the sandstone for an hour or so. Finally, we were able to loosen one stone which was about a foot square.

"Hey Lee, grab hold of the other side and help me work this stone out." We tugged and pulled and finally it pulled free.

A pungent stale odor poured out the open hole in the sandstone wall. It was pitch black inside the opening and I couldn't see a thing.

I turned to Lee saying,"I'm going back to the truck to get a flashlight; we've got to see what's behind that door."

I could feel the excitement as I trotted back to the truck. I reached the truck, jerked open the door and popped open the glove compartment. I fumbled through the mass of papers and junk I had collected in the glove box. I finally found the flashlight. I grabbed hold of it and it lit up.

I hadn't even touched the switch. The bulb was glowing brightly. I realized the bannerstone hanging against my chest was red hot. I had trouble concentrating on the bannerstone and Taza. I kept thinking about that darn sealed door.

Curiosity was killing me. The message from Taza was strong. So strong, that I couldn't ignore it even if I wanted to.

I slid into the passenger's side seat and closed my eyes and concentrated on the clutched Bannerstone.

With one foot on the running board and one on the ground, my mind finally cleared. Taza was sending me a message.

"Don't open the sealed door, it is booby trapped." Taza continued, "If it is opened, it will set off a huge explosion."

"The first room behind the door contains boxes of dynamite and barrels of gun powder."

"A detonator charge box is connected by a copper wire to set off the charge of explosives when the door is opened."

My thoughts went haywire. "How do you know about the cabin and the sealed door, I asked?"

Taza's message came back to me quickly. "Meet me at the back of the canyon tonight, twelve o'clock midnight, and I will fully explain, and bring Lee with you." I couldn't keep from thinking; Lee is going to be totally amazed when she lay's eye on that space ship.

The Bannerstone cooled immediately. I knew the conversation was over.

I grabbed the flashlight and ran back to the cabin. Lee had been working on the door with my pocket knife. I approached the hole where we had removed the stone and shined the light into the black opening.

I could see several oak barrels and some wooded boxes and I could just make out the faded writing on the boxes; "dynamite." The barrels were labeled, "Black Powder."

I shined the light as high as I could. My chin and cheek were pressed tightly against my arm which I had stuck through the hole holding the flashlight.

With my face tight against the sandstone, I caught a glimpse of a long copper wire hanging from the ceiling. That must be the trigger mechanism Taza talked about.

"Lee, come here and look at this."

"Here take the flashlight and look what's in here." Lee took the flashlight and poked her face to the hole. "Hell", Lee exclaimed, "it's old barrels and boxes; I was expecting to see some gold."

"Look closer Lee, those are not just old barrels, they're barrels of gunpowder and boxes of dynamite."

"This door is booby trapped."

"When the door is opened the gunpowder will explode."

"There's a detonator box in there and copper wire that sets off the off the explosion."

"The door only has to open a very small amount before the place blows sky high." Lee looked puzzled saying, "Why would anyone want to blow up the cabin unless they were hiding something and they wouldn't want anyone else to find?"

"I think you're right, I said."

"I'll bet that gunpowder and dynamite is protecting the gold treasure."

"Now the only question is how to disarm this thing without blowing us up with it."

"Lee, do you have a makeup mirror in your purse?" Lee answered, "Sure do, it's in my clutch purse laying over there by the door."

Lee walked over and picked up her purse and started opening compartments. "Here it is", she exclaimed. "Just don't mess up the makeup in my compact."

I looked at Lee with a, "I don't believe you said that." How can she be concerned with her makeup when we got a booby trapped door that's guarding a possible treasure of gold? That's a women I guess. I'll never understand how they think.

I opened the round compact. The mirror was surprisingly big. I held the mirror through the hole opening and looked as far back as I could. I took the flashlight and shined the beam into the mirror.

I could see the copper wire and something was resting on the inside door ledge. What a simple trigger system. When the door was opened, the wire would pull a weight off the ledge and it would fall on the detonator box handle and the charge would ignite the black gunpowder.

Sounds almost too simple, maybe they have a backup trigger? I continued to shine the flashlight on the mirror and moved them together to see if anything else was above the door.

There it was; a faded orange stick of dynamite tied to one end of a rope and the other to the copper wire.

I could see the wet seepage on the outside of the dynamite as if it were sweating. Natural nitro glycerin, that's what it was.

The dynamite was just hanging off a rock edge, up by the ceiling. "Lee, I see another darn booby trap; we don't dare jar anything around this door."

"Let's go around behind the cabin and see if we can find another way into this hidden room."

We moved around the side of the old sandstone cabin only to see the whole back of the cabin was built into a vertical rock hill side. The vines and the brush had completely covered the back of the cabin and hid the vertical rock face of the hill.

"Well Lee, we must really think carefully about that booby trap."

"That dynamite gets more dangerous as it ages because that nitro glycerin seeps out of it and collects like sweat beads on the outside cover."

"Any jar or sudden jolt or even a low frequency could set that stuff off and with all that black gun powder, they wouldn't find enough of us to ever know we'd been here."

Lee answered with a serious wide eyed look. "Ya, and if that gold is hid back there in that hill and there was that kind of explosion no one would ever find it."

I nodded my head in agreement. "I think that was their plan, but they had to have another way into there to get gold when they needed it."

"I'll bet there is another way into that sealed room." Lee answered, "These hills are solid sandstone rock so they could tunnel in a long way without having to worry about caving in".

"You know Lee, there are a lot of natural caves around here where surface water has seeped in and deteriorated the sandstone creating big holes in the sandstone."

"Let's look for a dry low spot on top of the hill where water might pool up and seep into the ground."

Lee and I hiked through the overgrown brush and tall prairie grass making our way to the top of the hill.

About twenty feet from the top there was a round flat area about the size of my truck where a large boulder stood.

We made our way through the prairie grass and around to the boulder and laid our hands on the smooth sandstone rock. It had some markings on it but they were so eroded they were not legible.

Lee spoke," I don't think anyone is going to move this rock to hide a cave entrance, it must weigh ten tons."

I answered back, "I think you're right Lee and I don't see any other candidate rocks up here or possible cave openings."

We headed back down towards the dry creek bed and hiked the dry bed towards the cabin until it disappeared as part of the prairie.

"Lee, one thing is sure, if there is another way into that back room it sure is hid well." Lee agreed saying, "If I were going to hide a big bunch of gold, I'd find a really good place too."

"Lee, we better get back to the cabin and put that stone back in the door opening."

"I wouldn't want some squirrel or raccoon getting in there and blowing the place up."

"It's getting late anyway and I'm starved to death. We walked back to the cabin.

It was a lot easier walking in the dry creek bed than it was through that tall grass.

We reached the cabin and stepped down onto the sandstone floor. It felt cool in the old cabin but projected a warm home like feeling. It must have been a great place to live when it was new.

I picked up the stone and slowly started working it back into the hole. It was kind of odd. Once the stone was back in place, you couldn't tell it had ever been pulled out. The sandstone hid the crack really well.

Lee and I went back to the truck. Lee clasped onto my hand, her warm hand said enough.

I turned the truck around, backing up and driving forward several times due to the ground having a huge outcrop of rocks more the size of small boulders. I finally got the truck turned around and we headed back out of the canyon.

The road was dusty as usual and we rolled up both windows to help keep some of the dust out.

I turned towards Lee, "I've got a favor to ask you Lee and I don't feel good about asking it." Lee blurted back with a big grin on her face, "If you want to take me to the back of the canyon and make love the answer is"....(There was a long hesitation), "not in this dusty truck", and then she laughed teasingly, like that was the best joke she'd ever heard.

"That wasn't exactly what I was going to ask you, but since you brought it up"........., (I hesitated a long time). We both broke into a good laugh.

"Seriously Lee," I want you to come back out here with me tonight at twelve o'clock midnight, to be exact."

"I've got something I need to show you and I won't tell you anymore about it, so don't ask."

Lee thought for a moment saying, "Well, you didn't have any trouble asking so I'll tell you straight out, "Yes", no questions asked, and I'll come ready for anything."

Lee continued, "Ya, I'm game, and not only that, it sounds mysterious and exciting and I hope you've thought of a way to get into that sealed room without blowing it up."

"No Lee", I answered, "I haven't, but I know there has to be another way into that room."

"When we come back tonight," I continued," We need to be sure and bring my five cell flashlight."

"We'll shine that bright light into the hole in the door; then go outside behind the cabin and see if we can see any light showing through a crack in the rock or something." Lee answered, "That sounds like a plan to me."

The road hadn't got any smoother or less dusty than it was when we drove in on it. It reminded me of what they called a corduroy road back in the late 1800's.

Ten

We pulled into my yard. Lee and I got out of the pickup and started toward the house. As soon as we reached the porch I could smell something cooking in the kitchen. It was Nora working her miracles in the kitchen and man, was I ever hungry. That tramping around in the canyon really gives you an appetite.

Nora spoke as we entered the kitchen. "I wondered when you all were going to get back."

"I figured Rolf's belly would be rubbing his backbone soon so I thought I'd better throw something together to eat."

Charlie was already sitting at the table reading the paper. A cup of coffee sat in front of him with the steam still rolling up out of the cup. When Nora made a cup of coffee, she made a "Hot" cup of coffee.

Nora said," You all sit down to the table; we're having pot luck tonight."

What that means; Nora cleans out the refrigerator and puts it all in one pot and slow cooks it for hours. It doesn't look too good but it tastes great.

We sat at the table talking. I ask Charlie," What time did Jack and Julie leave today?" Charlie answered, "Oh, they took off just after you and Lee had left."

"They wanted to get back home with those hay baler parts and get that baler back working."

I asked Charlie if he had ever been out to the box canyon on Doc Watson's Ranch. Charlie said, "Oh Ya," I grew up playing in that canyon." I almost fell out of my chair. "You what?" I grabbed the edge of the table with both hands and leaned over the table towards Charlie.

"Ya", Charlie said, my dad and mom used to go out there and fish in the creek and us kids played all over the canyon."

I was totally excited. "What about the old sandstone cabin, I asked?"

"That was my favorite hiding place", Charlie smiled as he leaned back in his chair. He knew he had us hooked and we would have to know everything he knew about that canyon.

He was right. "Charlie", I asked, "do you know of any cave opening around that old cabin?"

"As a matter of fact," Charlie leaned forward in his chair and tilted his head to the side as if in deep thought. The big hesitation was killing me. Finally, he reared back in his chair again.

"Ya, Charlie said, "You know where that creek makes a bend after it runs between them two hills and heads south?" Lee spoke up, "Ya, I know where that is." Charlie continued, "Well, in that bend was our old swimming hole."

"If you climb up the bank about, say, twenty yards, there is a big rock; probably the biggest one up there; stands about ten feet tall and about fifteen feet around."

"There's an animal path that leads around behind some big boulders and there's a big buzzard nest up there on top."

"You can't miss it because it smells like rotten animal carcass."

"It used to almost take your breath away".

"Well, in the hill side behind the buzzard nest, there used to be a small opening about two feet high and about six feet wide."

"You could just slid in if you lay on your stomach and dug away some of the dirt and rocks that had slid off the hill side because it was filling up the opening."

"It was pitch black in that cave."

"We took a carbide light one time, and went back in about fifty feet."

"It opened up into a large room."

"The room's walls were blackened from Indian camp fires and when you get at the back of the room, there's a hole that goes straight down."

Bannerstone 75

"You drop a rock in it and count to five before you hear it hit water; so it's a deep hole."

"We figured the creek probably run under the sandstone bluff and filled some of the cavities or there could be another spring feeding into the creek."

Charlie continued, "You know them carbide lights, they throw a pretty darn bright light." We used to wear them on our caps when we went coon hunting."

"Charlie get back to the cave," I asked. Charlie had a way of wandering off the subject and I wanted to hear about that cave.

"Oh ya", Charlie cleared his voice, "Well, one summer, years later, Nora and I had went up there a courting."

"It was a really hot late afternoon and we took a picnic lunch down by the old cabin, we spread a blanket out on a big sandstone rock under a cottonwood tree and were having a sweet time."

Nora reached across the table and hit Charlie on the shoulder saying, "You don't have to go into details." Charlie broke out a mischievous grin saying, "Well that's another story," and laughed with a flirting look towards Nora.

Charlie went on, "We had decided to take a walk down by the creek and I ended up showing Nora the buzzard's nest." A storm was coming up from nowhere quickly and the sky was turning dark grey."

"We didn't have time to get to the car so we took cover in the cave."

"Well the storm hit and we could hear the tree branches breaking from the high wind and then the rain came."

"It was one of them gully washers."

"Nora and I must have been in the cave about twenty minutes or so and we heard a loud rumbling noise."

"Some of the rocks on the side of the hill was sliding and falling outside the cave opening and it was starting to close the cave entrance."

"Nora and I made a mad dash for the opening and when we hit the partially closed opening we had to push rocks and mud to crawl out."

"I remember being peppered on the back with rain, mud, and rocks as we slid down the bank that led away from the cave."

"We hit the path running wide open all the way back to the car."

Nora excitedly spoke, "We sat in that car a long time it seemed."

"The rain and wind gusts shook the whole car and the rain blasted against the windows."

"I can remember that like it was yesterday," Nora went on to speak, "That sky was black and the clouds were rolling and there was probably a twister around, not too far away."

"The wind finally stopped and the rain with it."

"It was a kind of a ghostly colored sky and the sun started shining through the few clouds that were left in the sky overhead."

"Charlie and I decided to go back down and look at the creek because we could hear it roaring from all the rain."

"Well, when we got back to the creek we watched the limbs and muddy water rolling them down the creek and out of sight."

Charlie broke in. "Ya, that's when we decided to go back to the cave."

"We climbed the slippery bank about half way up and low and behold, the cave entrance was completely closed off."

"It just wasn't there anymore."

"That mud and rock slide had it covered completely and it was a darn good thing we got out of that cave when we did or we'd been goners."

I looked across the table at Lee. She was still sitting on the edge of her chair grabbing every word. Lee burst out, "Rolf, let's take some shovels and go check out that cave."

Before I could say anything, Charlie spoke up, "Whoa girl that was a long time ago and probably half that hill side is sitting on top of that cave entrance by now, and that's a dangerous place."

"Lot's of strange stories come out of that area and bye the way, the Indians called that cave, "Devils Hole," and for good reason."

I could see the determination in Lee's eyes. To tell her no about something was like throwing gasoline on a fire, she for sure was going to do it.

I chirped in to avoid an argument between Lee and Charlie.

"I think it would be fun to just go out there and see where the cave was." Lee looked at me hard. I gave her a little wink of the eye and she caught on to what was happening. She slid back in her chair biting her lip.

During supper, Nora and Charlie talked about the canyon and some of the stories and superstitions surrounding it. I started to realize now why not many people visited the place.

One of Charlie's stories that stuck in my mind, told the canyon was haunted by old Indian ghost's and that people that went in there at night, wouldn't be the same again and they didn't live long after they seen the ghosts. The way Charlie could tell a story, you believed it, no matter how far out it sounded.

Lee and I excused ourselves from the table and went out to the front porch swing. The evening was nice.

The sun had already moved below the horizon, but the sunlight still reflected off the clouds with beautiful pinks and blues laced with gold.

Lee snuggled up next to me on the porch swing and placed her hand on one side of my neck and pulled us together, our lips touching in a beautiful soft sweet kiss. I looked into her big green eyes. They were as green as a spring wheat field.

Lee spoke softly, "You know Rolf"; I think I'm falling in love with you."

"Not the puppy love kind, but the deep everlasting, can't do without you, kind of love." She had me almost in a trance. All I could do was kiss her sweet lips again and again.

That instant, we heard the screen door open. It was Charlie coming out on the porch as you might have guessed it; to talk.

Charlie sat down on the porch steps and leaned back on his elbows. "You know," Charlie started out, "I am looking forward to getting our house done and getting moved in; but I'm sure going to miss this place."

"There's a warm, homey feeling about this place and it just wants you to relax and enjoy all the things God has provided us."

"It's hard to find that in a place and I just hope our new house will have that feeling about it."

I looked at Lee and smiled saying, "Ya, I can surely agree with you on that."

Nora came out on the porch and sat down beside Charlie and we talked about the weather and world events.

Eventually we got around to the subject of the old Indian skirt Lee had bought from Milo Boles in Uniontown.

Lee and I both were tempted to tell them about the map Lee had found in the skirt pocket but something told us to keep that to ourselves.

Charlie slowly rose up off the porch steps saying, "Nora, let's hit the hay, morning comes too soon and we got a big day tomorrow over at the house." Nora took his hand and got up saying, "Goodnight you two Love birds," giving her smile of approval.

Lee and I sat swinging gently back and forth on the porch swing. I said to Lee, "Are you still ready to go out to the canyon tonight?" Lee spoke up, "sure am, you couldn't get away without me, but could you tell me why we need to go out there tonight or is it still a surprise?"

"Lee", I said, "I would rather wait till we get out there."

"Ok," Lee said. "I'm ready to leave anytime."

"I just need to get my purse and change shoes and I'll get that five cell flashlight of yours."

"I'll be here on the porch waiting", I answered. Lee was through the door and up the stairs in a flash. I sat on the porch swing gently swinging to and fro, thinking how to explain to Lee what we were about to witness tonight.

Lee was on the porch and ready to go. We hopped into the truck, ground a gear getting it in reverse and we were off to the canyon.

We drove toward the west. The sky was clear as a bell and the stars shown bright horizon to horizon, 360 degrees around. What a huge sky. "Lee, it's a good time to tell you what we're going to do out here tonight."

Lee answered, "Its Taza isn't it?"

"Yes", I answered, "but not only Taza, it's the space ship."

"They are going to meet with us tonight at the box canyon at midnight and they are driving a space ship."

"Be braced to see something you can't believe exists."

"I've seen it a couple of times up close and it's awesome."

"It doesn't even look like it could fly, but talk about flying, "wow."

"In a blink of an eye, it can be gone out of sight."

Lee spoke, "Oh Rolf, I'm trembling with excitement just hearing you talk about it."

"I hope I don't faint or something when I see it."

"Don't do that," I exclaimed, "I can handle only one thing at a time and I might overload and faint too." We both had to laugh at the thought of us both passed out with Taza looking on.

We pulled into the canyon and drove along the narrow road towards the cliffs at the back of the canyon. As we got close to the canyon wall, I could see the outline of the top ridge along the wall. We parked the truck and I looked at my watch. It was fifteen minutes till twelve O'clock.

Lee and I pushed open the truck doors and got out. I went around to Lee's side of the truck and we both leaned back against the front fender and watched the sky with great anticipation.

"How big is this space ship," Lee asked? "It's pretty big, hard to say, but you'll see it soon enough."

"Taza told me that this is just a landing craft, their mother ship is docked outside our atmosphere."

We continued to lean against the fender and studied the clear starry sky. I glanced at my watch again and it was twelve O'clock.

I looked up and saw a circle of lights moving towards us. Lee gasp, "holy shit", she let out a burst and then she froze not saying another word or moving.

That was my reaction the first time I seen it. It moved even closer, you couldn't hear a sound as the craft sat hovering about ten feet off the ground. Three legs with dish shaped pads slowly extended out of the vehicle's rim section and moved down until each pad touched the uneven ground. A blue haze exhausted from holes under the rim.

The craft sat motionless and silent until the blue lights under the saucer rim went dim. A large round tube extended straight down from under the craft till it touched the ground. The tube side rotated open.

There was Taza standing in the opening being silhouetted by the blue back lighted tube. She walked towards Lee and me.

Lee had grabbed hold of the truck door mirror and wasn't about to turn loose. I got Lee's hand and started to walk toward Taza, but Lee was still frozen. I put my arm around Lee and whispered, "It's OK Lee, come on let's meet Taza." Lee turned loose the mirror and we proceeded toward Taza.

Taza reached out putting her arm around Lee and gave her a big hug saying, "I feel like I have known you for a long time."

Taza turned to me; I gave her a big hug and a gentle kiss on the neck. It was great seeing Taza again. There is so much I'd like to know and understand about space travel and the universe, but how do I go about getting this information? All of a sudden, I could feel the bannerstone getting hot and a single thought overpowered my mind, "be more specific".

Taza started laughing out loud saying, "One of the reasons I needed to see you; you've just discovered." I looked at Taza puzzled, trying to understand what she had said.

"To activate the Bannerstone," Taza said, "You must address the Bannerstone with a question."

"It has been programmed in that manner after we studied your most natural method of seeking information."

I was totally taken back by Taza's statement. "You mean to tell me that anything I want to know, all I have to do is ask the Bannerstone and it will put a mental answer in my mind?"

Taza nodded her head yes, saying, "depending on the nature of your question, some portion of the answer will go into the conscience mind and some into the sub-conscience mind."

"Some questions may have complex or compound definition type answers, and cannot be processed into the conscience portion of the brain and therefore is transferred to the sub-conscience."

Taza continued, "Your next anticipated question is, "How do you retrieve the information out of your sub-conscience?"

"You must meditate focusing on the single subject question."

Taza went on to say, "This will take a great amount of practice but as you develop your self assurance and self confidence; you will have the power within you to perform this function."

I felt really confused about this mind consciousness. Taza is going to have to go through that explanation again. I want to understand everything about how this Bannerstone works.

That's one thing that really bugs me about Taza, she has a habit of talking about things I never thought about and expects me to know exactly what she's talking about. I guess it's just me but, I don't really like someone talking over my head. Anyway, back to the matters at hand.

Taza was talking with Lee and Lee was asking more questions per minute than I thought possible.

"Taza", I broke in, "you mentioned that there was something else you had to see us about?" Taza spoke in a very serious voice. "Yes, it's a favor I must ask of both of you." I answered back, "Sure Taza, just ask."

Lee chimed in, "sure, what is it you need?" Taza started off talking about the planet they were visiting when her Father took sick. Taza continued, "I told you Father was collecting mineral samples; those samples were really a specific type of gold which is only found on planet Plura and on Earth."

"You are probably aware that gold is specific to the region that it is mined."

"For instance, your Black Hills gold has a pink color."

"California gold, Colorado gold and Carolina gold, all have slight different molecular makeup."

"African gold is completely different than the gold mined in the America's."

"In the drive circuits of our mother ship, we require the type of gold found on Plura and only found in the Carolina gold."

"When we were on Plura, our mother ship encountered a solar flare that penetrated our energy deflector shields and blew the primary drive circuits."

"We cannot return to home without the use of our primary drives."

"We were quite fortunate to escape the flare and only by utilizing the rouge energy from the flare were we able to encounter break free gravity status from Plura." Lee and I stood silent and amazed as Taza continued. "We have scanned the Carolina Appalachian area and the Blue Ridge Mountain ranges for gold traces, but due to the high concentration of Franklinite in that area's earth surface, our scanners are unreliable."

I had to ask, "Taza, what is Franklinite?" Taza answered, "It is a mineral, black in color and has the identical crystal shape of diamond and is magnetic."

"It is mined for use in smelting of plumbum or Lead."

"It is found primarily in the southern mountain ranges in North

America."

Taza then got back to her situation. "We have been scanning the surface areas of planet Earth for any trace of this rare type of gold and were not successful until yesterday."

"We picked up a positive find in this area."

"We since have narrowed the scan to the cabin area you were at earlier today."

"When we ran a multi-beam ultrasonic scan on the cabin, we were able to see the interior of the room behind the cabin."

"I realized the danger to you and that's why I contacted you immediately."

"We detected explosives in the cabin area so we ran an analysis and found gunpowder, dynamite and nitroglycerin formation."

"The nitroglycerin is completely unstable."

"We have various techniques for drilling or boring into the room but none of our techniques fall within the stability level of the nitroglycerin."

I broke in, "so what you're saying is that you don't have a way to get into that room without setting off the nitro?" "That's correct," Taza answered, "We can only work by dark of night, so not to be detected, where you have the ability to explore by daylight."

"Taza, I've got to know, Lee blurted out, "Is there really gold in there?" Taza turned, "more gold than you can imagine," she answered. Lee let out a squeal of joy.

Taza began to speak again, "We were very fortunate that when we ran the multi-beam ultrasonic scan, we ran it on high frequency, had we scanned the nitroglycerin with low frequency, we would have exploded it."

"We desperately need that gold to repair the circuitry in our drive engines."

"It means our survival." Taza grasp my hand, her desperation showed.

"Taza, I said, "Lee and I think we know another way into that room."

I went on to tell Taza about Lee's father and mother and the cave they knew of by the creek but had been covered over by a landslide. I gave Taza the approximate location of the cave entrance.

Taza stated that they would check it out tonight using Umar rovers to remove the debris.

I asked, "What are Umar rovers?" Taza answered, "They are unmanned-articulating-rovers."

"We developed them to mine minerals in areas where conditions like weather, atmosphere, temperature, or radiation is not conducive to mankind."

Lee spoke up, "They better be gentle on moving that rock and dirt if that nitro is that unstable." Taza assured Lee that they would take all the necessary precautions.

It was almost one A.M. when I looked at my watch. Lee and I needed to get back home, grab some shut eye so we can be back out here early tomorrow morning.

We told Taza the plan and she agreed. Taza held out both hands, grasping my hand with one and Lee's hand with the other.

Taza looked at us deeply, speaking to our minds, not uttering a word from her mouth, "See you both tomorrow and we are deeply appreciative, thank you." She turned and walked back to the craft. The tube rotated open, she stepped in and the tube retracted up into the bottom of the craft.

It was gone in a split second. Not a sound of any kind, only a small streak of blue light was visible for the blink of an eye.

Eleven

Lee and I talked the whole way back to the house about everything that had occurred. It was incredible and still hard to believe. We didn't even notice the dust was fogging up in the truck.

We arrived home and crept into the house with our shoes off so not to wake anyone and went directly to our beds. We were both totally exhausted from today's ordeals.

The alarm clock was almost jumping off the night stand beside my bed when I finally got awake enough to shut it off. I lay there in bed thinking about what we had ahead of us today.

I heard Lee stirring around. I called out, "Hey Lee, you up to stay up or just temporarily?" She pushed open my bed room door saying, "Does this look like temporary?"

She had her hands on both hips, dressed in her tight blue jeans, black t-shirt, and cowgirl boots. I'd say she was ready to ride.

She walked over and sat down on the side of my bed and leaned over me. I thought she was going to lay a sweet kiss on me. Instead she pushed her hands under my arm pits and started tickling me.

I went wild, screaming and hollering and kicking. She knew I was ticklish under the arms beyond my control. We rolled around over the bed; I had to get her fingers out of my ribs. I got one hand free and got her in the ribs and started tickling her.

She was screaming and hollering when Nora stepped into the doorway. "What's going on up here, it sounds like you're going to come through the floor and land in the kitchen."

We both sat up in bed. Nora went on saying, "Breakfast is ready if you two can pull your selves together and Rolf, you better get some clothes on."

I looked down and Lee was holding up the bed covers giving Nora a clean eyeball shot of me underneath the covers. Lee laughed historically. She knew she had embarrassed me to no end.

I wrapped the covers around me tight as Lee hopped off the bed in a dead run downstairs.

Nora turned to me saying, "Best you wear sleeping clothes while we're staying here in the house"; she was dead serious.

I felt like I had just got a whipping from my mom. I answered back, "I'm sorry Nora, and I'll do just that."

I got into my Levis and shirt and hurried down stairs to breakfast. Nora had fixed pancakes and each one was big as the plate. Nothing like pancakes and bacon cooking in the kitchen to start the day off right.

We have an exciting day ahead of us, I thought, as I looked over the big breakfast in front of me. Lee nor I said a word about the cabin or anything we experienced last night and we sure wasn't mentioning Taza.

After breakfast, Lee and I took off for the canyon. We were both anxious to find out what progress Taza had made during the night.

It seemed like forever to get to the turnoff that led to the canyon.

Finally, we saw the pile of sandstone posts along side the road. The canyon road will be just ahead. I swung the truck onto the dirt road and as usual the dust was filling the truck cab to the point you could taste the flat powder dust in your mouth.

We pulled into the canyon and drove back around the high banks to the cabin. Lee and I got out of the truck and walked toward the cabin.

The morning sun was already warming the prairie grass and flowers; giving off a unique odor that you can't find any place else. It was a good smell that made you feel free and you knew that only God could make a smell that would give you such a fulfilling feeling.

Lee opened the cabin door slowly as if she might see a ghost. "I don't see any trace of where anyone has been here since we were here yesterday", Lee exclaimed.

I answered back, "Ya, let's go around behind the cabin and down

Bannerstone

to the creek to see if they actually did some digging."

I followed Lee out the door and down the steep path to the creek. We walked along the creek; around the bend and there it was.

A hole in the side of the bank above the creek you could ride a horse in. I was expecting a small crawl space not mine shaft opening.

I looked around for a dirt pile where they had dug out the opening but there wasn't even a rock lying around. "What do you suppose they did with the dirt", I asked Lee? Lee had already started into the mine. She turned saying, "I don't know, but I've never seen walls so slick and smooth; there's hardly a mark on these walls."

It got dark in the mine really quick. One thing was really different in this mine; the shape of the mine shaft itself. It was a perfect triangle. The floor was wide and the walls went up to a point, meeting in the center of the roof.

I guess that eliminated any wood support timbers that would normally be used to hold up the roof to prevent a cave-in.

"Lee, we need a flashlight, it's black as a ace of spades in here; I'm going back to the truck and get the five cell flashlight."

Lee answered back quickly, "Not without me; this mine is spooky."

We hustled back to the truck, grabbed the flashlight and ran back to the mine.

We entered the mine shaft out of breath; flashed the light on the mine walls. They were black and so smooth they reflected the light like a dark mirror; almost like they had been burnt. I asked in amazement, "How did they dig this darn thing; I have never seen anything like this in my life."

I had laid my hand on the bannerstone because it was hanging outside my shirt swinging as I walked; it started heating up and the answer to my question came flooding out of my brain like it couldn't wait to get out. "Molecular compression; the use of a crystal triangular tool which emits a frequency wave length that compresses dirt and stone as the vibratory process sizes the hole based on the energy level you wish to exert; thus will solidify the wall surface to prevent collapse."

"Lee, I know how this bannerstone works and it is awesome."

"I just ask a question while holding on to it and I get a mental answer to my question."

"It's a carry along encyclopedia."

"Boy, am I ever going to have fun with this."

Lee answered back, "Ya, and like Taza said, you better use it for only good, moral reasons and that probably eliminates most of your thoughts, so you'll be limited to where you can use it."

"Very funny Lee, I can think of all kinds of nitty, gritty uses for this."

We walked deeper into the cave and you could feel the mine floor going up hill steeply. The light from the flashlight bounced off the slick black walls like a reflector and lit up the whole mine shaft.

Suddenly the mine shaft stopped. There was a three foot circle of one inch holes drilled into the back wall of the mine.

I shined the flashlight into one of the holes. The drilled holes went all the way through into an open area on the other side.

Lee and I looked carefully into each hole and in one hole we could see the light reflecting off a gold colored object. Lee spoke in almost a whisper," do you think this is the hidden Indian gold?"

"Could be, I answered in an excited voice, they sure went to a lot of trouble to hid whatever is in there."

I continued," there must be a reason why Taza didn't open the hole up all the way rather then just drilling holes through the wall?" Lee agreed saying," Let's get out of here and contact Taza and find out what happened."

"That's a great idea Lee; you know with those explosives behind that wall we can't be too careful, even the bannerstone frequency might set it off."

We made our way back out the mine shaft. I grasped hold of the bannerstone and ask, "How do I contact Taza?" The bannerstone started heating up immediately. Taza answered asking if we had been to the mine?

I answered back that we had been in the mine and discovered the holes drilled in the back wall and I asked what the next thing we needed to do.

Taza answered," some of the Carolina gold and Indian artifacts are located against the wall where we were drilling."

"Due to a box of dynamite sitting against the solid portion of the circle, the box is actually setting on top of one of the artifacts; therefore we could not drill anymore without the possibility of setting off the explosives."

"We need the gold too desperately to risk destroying it." Taza ask for suggestions on how to remove the rock circle without using ultrasonic frequency.

A light bulb lit in my head. "I have an idea that might work."

"I remember hearing how my ancestors used to cut sandstone into squares for building houses and also sandstone fence posts."

"They drilled holes in a straight line and would take wood cedar plugs and drive them into the drilled holes."

"Then they poured water on the plugs which would swell up and crack the sandstone in a long straight line between each hole."

"So if we drive cedar plugs in each of the holes and soaked them with water we could crack the rock between each hole and pry the rock out gently from the wall."

Taza responded saying, "that's a brilliant idea, but I'd like to run a material analysis to understand the fracture characteristics of this particular sandstone with expansion rates of dry and wet cedar wood."

There was a mental silence. My thoughts were wide open in thinking about Taza's response. Then the silence broke, Lee asked, "well, what's she thinking?" I motioned with my hand for Lee to get hold of the bannerstone.

She laid her hand on mine just as Taza was sending her thoughts back. Her thoughts were exciting and actually lifted my eyebrow as she explained the factors that supported the method of removing the sandstone.

She asked that we drive the tapered cedar plugs in every other hole and then throw multiple buckets of water on the entire wall thoroughly saturating the wall area.

Lee spoke, "I saw an old galvanized bucket in the cabin and we can get water from the creek."

"Ya", I answered, and there is a bunch of old cedar trees on the other side of the creek and I got an axe in the truck."

Lee and I took off to get the axe and the bucket. After picking up what we thought we needed, we walked along the creek looking for a place to cross.

We had only went about fifty yards when right in front of us stood a half dead cedar standing along side an Osage orange tree or hedge tree as we called them.

The limbs on the cedar were wound among the hedge limbs and entwined to the point the trees were inseparable. The great thing was that the cedar limbs were just the right size that we needed for plugs.

It was tough climbing up the hedge tree as the thorns dug in and brought blood with every scratch. Lee handed me the axe and I started chipping away at the cedar. I'm glad in one way, the cedar and hedge had grown up together because I would have never been able to climb that darn tree.

I cut off the limbs and Lee piled them up till it looked like we had plenty of potential plugs. We trimmed up the limbs and cut the plugs off making sure they would reach all the way through the wall.

"We'll take the plugs back to the mine and size them to fit the holes", I said to Lee. I picked up the arm load of plugs and Lee picked up the bucket, axe, and tools and headed back to the mine.

It's a good thing I kept the fence mending tools with me in the truck; you never know when you're going to need tools. Between the two of us, we are loaded down. I knew what pack mules felt like when old prospectors started off with them loaded down with mining supplies.

We trudged to the cave and laid out all of our tools on the cave floor next to the back wall. I got out my pocket knife and axe and started whittling on sizing the plugs to fit the holes.

Much to my surprise, all the holes were the same size, so I made a master sized plug and made all the plugs to match it. After about two hours we had enough plugs to fill every other hole. We pushed a plug into the top hole and took the hammer and gently tapped the plug in till it was super tight. Then worked our way around and down every other hole till the plugs were in place.

I went back around and give each plug another light rap. The plugs sounded with a deep thud as the hammer slapped against them.

Now it was time to soak them down with water. Lee was already down at the creek scooping up a bucket of water as I finished moving the tools away from the wall.

Bannerstone   91

She was back with the water in a heart beat saying, "Stand back, I'm going to blast that wall with water." I teasingly responded, "I wish you wouldn't use that word "blast", right now, Let's say "drench" the wall with water." We both laughed with Lee saying, "Ya, it's a better use of words at this particular time."

For the next half hour we took turns going to the creek and returning to the wall and drenching the entire wall with water till every plug seemed soaking wet.

"I guess we'll just have to wait now till it cracks, Lee exclaimed."

"Ya, I guess so", I answered, but it'll probably take a while and we'll have to put more water on them about every hour till the sandstone cracks." Lee looked at me with her famous "you've got to be kidding" look.

"Lee, I'm not kidding; those plugs have got to be kept wet so they will swell as much as possible." Lee asked in an almost disappointing tone, "Just how long is it going to be before we can get through that wall?" I answered back,"I really don't know exactly, but it won't be till tomorrow at the earliest."

"I'm going to have to wait till tomorrow to see that gold," Lee blurted out?"

"Yes, you didn't expect this to happen immediately did you?" Lee answered, "I never split rocks with a wood plug before so how the Hell should I know?"

I knew Lee was getting to the end of her rope so I changed the subject real fast. "Lee, let's get out of here and go get some something to eat; it's been a long time since breakfast". Lee agreed.

It was starting to get dusk outside as the sun was setting over the hills and across the wide open prairie. Lee and I had walked up to the top of the rim that encircled the canyon. It was a beautiful view; you could see the horizon off to the west with the gold, pink, and blue all laced together as only God could paint such a picture.

"You know Lee, I'll bet that Indian gold in that mine isn't any prettier than this sky." Lee agreed with a nod and laid her head over on my shoulder. I continued, "And do you know something else; this gold is so important to Taza and her people, I don't want any of it for myself; I'm happy just to be here in the middle of Kansas with a sweet girl sitting on a rock watching the sunset; it just can't get any better than this."

We sat there looking at the sun slowly sink below the horizon and talked about the prospects of tomorrow.

"Lee we better be heading back home; it'll be dark in a half an hour and I think I've got enough gas to get home."

Lee turned and looked me in the eye; "you better have enough gas to get home or you'll have to carry me."

"I've been walking and tugging tree limbs and everything else all day and I'm not about to walk even if you do run out of gas."

"Now Lee, you know you would like to take a moonlight stroll under the stars with me holding your hand and whispering sweet nothings in your ear."

"Rolf," Lee exclaimed, "You're the only person I know that can take a catastrophe and turn it into a fun thing to do." We had got back to the truck and started home. Lee kept an eye on the gas gauge all the way back to town like she expected the truck to suck its last drop of gas from the tank at any moment.

We pulled into the driveway and drove up next to the garage and parked the truck. The porch light came on immediately and Nora came out on the porch. "If you had been two minutes later you would have missed supper because I was ready to throw it out to the dogs."

I could tell Nora was a bit bent out of shape by her tone of voice but Lee and I both laughed under our breath because we both knew if we hadn't got in by midnight, she'd still have supper ready.

Nora had fixed fried chicken for dinner today and warmed it up with all the trimmings. I never knew warmed up food could taste so darn good.

Nora had to keep slipping in little questions to find out where we'd been and what we'd been doing all day. Looking at the dirt on our clothes, she probably thought we'd been messing around in a pig pen.

We told her we had went out to the box canyon and hiked all around and explored some of the area. We kept dodging some of her questions because we couldn't dare tell them what was really happening out there.

After supper, Lee and I did the dishes and ran Nora out of the kitchen to give her a rest and to join Charlie on the front porch.

Lee and I finished cleaning up the kitchen and went out the back kitchen door. We walked out to the field road that ran behind the garage.

I laid my hand on the Bannerstone and thought; where is Taza? Taza answered immediately. She was at the mine and she was injecting the cedar plugs with an expansion resin compound which will speed the natural process of cellulose swelling and increase the cell expansion pressure.

The center circle will not only be ready for removal tomorrow morning, but will be shattered by multiple cracks making removal of the circle area much easier.

Taza also reminded us to be extremely careful; the nitro glycerin is unstable to a greater degree than initially measured and will react to any low frequency vibration.

Taza will meet us at the mine tomorrow night at nine o-clock, Earth time, and reminded me that tomorrow will be a very important time for all of us.

Boy, when you ask a question, you really get an answer; and she says she studied me so she could talk on my understanding level. I'm not too sure of that sometimes. Anyway, it sounds like tomorrow morning we'll be able to take that circle of rock out piece by piece rather than one big chunk.

I have been concerned about how we were going to move that big center out without possibly having it hit the floor with a thud and risking an explosion.

Lee was anxious to find out what Taza had said. We continued walking up the dirt road and I told Lee all about what Taza had said. Naturally, Lee had more questions than I had answers.

"Lee, the next time I talk with Taza, you're going to hang on to that Bannerstone with me and just maybe, between the two of us, we can really understand everything she tells us." Lee spoke up, "I'd like that."

We strolled hand in hand down the old dirt road away from the house toward the moonlit fields which looked like a giant ocean of water. The lack of wind seemed to make the tall prairie grass sigh a relief of not having to brace itself against the constant blowing of the daytime wind.

Lee turned toward me. The moon light reflected off her cheeks and forehead lighting up every expression on her face.

"You know", she began; I had really and truly believed that God had put life only on the Earth and the rest of the Universe was just barren rock and sand."

"Although the Bible says's he created Heaven and Earth and all things."

"I really didn't think he put people on other Planets just like us."

"I know what you mean," I answered, "but who's to know that maybe God put people on other Planets thousands of years before we got here and maybe we were brought here by space explorer's to start a new World; all according to God's plan."

Lee was in deep thought as she stood still in the middle of the dirt road looking up at the moon.

"Yes", Lee said, "I bet there is a whole lot of Planets up there that would support life and I bet Taza would know and I'm going to ask her tomorrow night when we see her."

"Ya", I agreed, "She might have a whole new idea on how we got here and who knows, maybe this Bannerstone might be chucked full of answers and all we have to do is ask the right questions."

"We better be heading back to the house, I added, or Nora and Charlie will be sending out a search party to find us."

Lee agreed saying, "Yes but here is a little something for you; you little space animal."

Lee turned toward me and threw both arms around my neck and pulled me up tight against her. We kissed and held each other as there was never going to be another moment like this.

Lee had really gotten hold of my heart and I felt like I wanted to keep her close to me forever. I've never felt this way before about anyone. It's like I don't have any control of what I should do and the urge to do what I want to do is almost overwhelming.

I want to make love to her right here in the middle of the dirt road under the moonlight, like two foxes in a forest fire.

I finally got hold of my better senses. I didn't have any protection with me and I'll bet Lee would get pregnant in a flash.

All the consequences flashed before my eyes. Now was not the time, so I held Lee close and whispered in her ear, "I love you sweet thing."

I think Lee was disappointed that I didn't at least go a little further with her. She looked up at me with the sweetest, most innocent look saying, "You can do anything you like." Boy, would I ever like, I thought.

I answered, "Lee we need to cool it a little bit, I think the moon has gotten to us both and I don't want to do something we might both be sorry for tomorrow." Lee looked at me saying," You are right Rolf, and I shouldn't have said, you can do anything". "What I meant was, almost anything." Lee let out a big hearty laugh as she grabbed my hand in hers and we started walking back towards the house.

Twelve

Nora and Charlie had gone to bed, only a light in the kitchen separated the house from the night.

"Lee, I said, tomorrow is going to be another exciting day."

"You know we'll have to be super careful opening that cave because there might be other booby traps in there besides the dynamite."

"Ya, Lee answered," my uncle told me about how the enemy in world war two would put bombs in old weight scales because they knew every American would weigh themselves when they seen a weight scale; so when they stepped onto the scale, the bomb would explode." I shook my head saying, "It's sometimes our old habits can get us into trouble real fast." "Ya, Lee said, I happen to know some people sleep in the buff, naked as new born birds and if they ever had to get out of the house in a hurry, they'd be in a big heap of trouble." I looked at Lee, "you wouldn't be referring to someone like me would you?" Lee grinned saying, "yes possibly."

"Well one question comes to mind real quickly, how do you know I sleep in the nude?"

"Well", Lee said, "one hot night I just happened to walk past your room and I heard a noise so I opened the door and the moon was shinning brightly and someone was laying in bed stark naked but it was too dark to see their face but the rest of them was pretty visible."

Lee laughed big time because she knew she had really embarrassed me. I asked," are you kidding me or did that really happen?"

Lee answered, "You'll never know for sure will you." Lee turned and walked towards her room laughing as she said, "goodnight," in a melodious voice.

The sound of a rooster crowing woke me up. The bed felt warm and cozy. I rolled over in bed and pulled the covers up to my neck. At that moment I realized I was laying on something. I reached under me and pulled out a sheet of paper.

I lifted it up to the light to read the writing scribbled on the paper. It read; "you should really start locking your door."

That darned Lee had slipped into my bedroom last night and slipped that note under the covers. I jumped up out of bed, slipped into my pants and headed down the hall to Lee's bedroom.

I grabbed hold of the door knob and swung the door wide open. Lee instantly rose up in bed with a surprised look on her face and holding the bed covers tight around her breasts.

"What in the world are you doing coming into my bedroom without knocking, Lee asserted?" I stood there dumb founded.

I couldn't believe she said that. "Lee, you are really the one to talk about someone coming into a room unannounced."

"I suppose you don't know how this note got into my bed last night?" Lee started grinning like a possum in a paw paw patch. "Ok", she said, "I guess I had that one coming."

She went on saying," you know you almost got me in trouble last night?"

"Now how was that", I answered. "Well", Lee hesitating as she looked for the right words to say. "I was up getting a drink of water last night and I walked past your door and I got this thought of how funny it would be to slip under the covers with you and then wake you up."

"Well, I was ready to slip into bed with you and I realized you might be sleeping in the nude so I decided to just write you a note."

"Lee, you are one of the craziest people I have ever known."

"You want to slip into bed with me, and then because you think I'm nude, you leave me a note."

"Lee, honestly, I've got to think about this one for a while."

"What would make the difference whether I had sleeping clothes on or not, they wouldn't have been on long if you got under the covers with me?" Lee looked shocked as if she hadn't thought that I might not have jumped out of bed and ran.

"Lee, you know there is a limit to a man's ability to resist temptation."
Lee came back, "I thought you were above temptation or I would have
worked a lot harder on you." Lee was smiling mischievously.

"Lee, we've got a big day ahead of us at the cave so I'll see you
downstairs at the breakfast table."

It didn't take Lee long to dress as she almost beat me downstairs.
Nora had her usual big farmer's breakfast on the table. I could smell
the bacon cooking long before I got close to the kitchen. She sat a big
pan of biscuits, hot from the oven in front of me. The smell was still
rolling off these beautiful brown biscuits. It's a good thing Nora isn't
my age, I'd snap her up in a heartbeat just for her cooking.

We finished breakfast without any discussion of our plan to go to
the cabin. Lee and Nora knocked out washing the dishes and cleaning
up the kitchen.

Lee came out on the porch where Charlie and I were discussing the
weather forecast for the week.

"Rolf", Lee remarked, "you promised to show me that old cabin
today." I answered back," Ya Lee, let's go."

"I need to get gas in the truck and we'll be on our way." Nora broke
in, "if you're going out to the cabin, you need to take a picnic lunch
so if you'll wait a minute, I'll throw some stuff together so you won't
starve." Nora is an angel after my own heart; she's always looking out
for everyone.

In a matter of minutes Nora was back to the front porch with a
paper bag bulging with food and a mason jar of ice water. I gave her
a big hug saying; "you might have just saved my life." She pushed me
back with a big smile," best you get going, if you're going."

Lee and I hopped into the truck and drove down to the gas station.
Don Wilkins run the gas station and never missed a chance to pump
our gas and talk to Lee. He always spends entirely too much time
washing the windshield while he tells her some wild story about
something that had just happened to him. I really think he's laying an
eyeball on Lee in those tight jeans instead of cleaning the bugs off the
windshield.

We finally got gassed up and got on the road. I looked over at Lee;
"Lee, Don back there at the station, did you ever date him?"

"Ya", Lee answered," We went out a couple of times." There was a long silence. "If you don't mind me asking Lee, why did you quit going with him?"

"No, I don't mind", Lee answered. "He and Johnny Milson were sharing a room together at the Wilson Boarding house and every time I called over there to talk to him, Jean Cox answered his phone."

"I think she stayed over at their place more than she did at her own house."

"You know Rolf, she had a reputation of being wild."

"I told Don I didn't like their arrangement and I told him I didn't want to see him anymore."

"That was it", I asked? "Ya", Lee answered, "that was it; I don't go out with guys that have loose women on the side."

"So watch your step Rolf." Lee laughed with a tone that told me she was sending me a message behind that laugh.

"You know Lee, that Johnny Milson and Jean Cox are engaged to be married?"

"I don't care, Lee said, I didn't like the arrangement." I could tell by the tone of her voice Lee really didn't want to talk about it anymore.

We turned off the main road onto the canyon dirt road and drove back to the cabin. "Let's check out the cabin first and then the cave; what do you think Lee?"

"Sounds like a plan", Lee answered. "I'll get the flashlight and I need to get the tire iron in case we need to pry some rocks loose."

"Good idea Rolf."

We slammed the truck doors with enthusiasm and started toward the cabin with tools in hand. Lee was really fired up this morning. She was walking in a half run pace ahead of me. I had to finally tell her to slow down so I could keep up.

In front of us, nestled in the prairie grass, vine covered and backed up against the sandstone rock, stood the little old cabin.

I turned to Lee saying, "I still think this would be a great place to fix up to its original condition and live here." Lee looked up at me grinning,"Ya, I could live here with you; is this some kind of a proposal by chance?" My face turned totally red. Lee had done it to me again. She never misses a chance to catch me in a serious moment to discuss getting hitched. "No", I answered," I was only thinking of house construction ideas out loud."

Lee pushed the squeaky cabin door open. Everything looked undisturbed with no sign that anyone else had been here. We went out of the cabin and took the trail that led along the creek and up the path to the cave entrance.

We walked into the cave, Lee switched on the flashlight. The light reflected off the triangle shaped walls lighting up the whole cave. We reached the back wall. Lee directed the flashlight beam onto the cedar plugged holes in the wall.

"Great," I shouted, there must be a thousand cracks between the cedar plugs. Some of the sandstone had already chipped out and fell to the cave floor. Lee held the flashlight and I began prying away at the rock with the tire iron. The cedar plugs had done the trick. The sandstone started falling out in big hunks. The hole was enlarging fast.

Then it happened. A large chunk had lodged itself in the upper left hand corner and I seen it start to fall.

I reached out with both arms and lunged forward; the whole top section fell flat on my arms.

I don't know which was loudest, the crash of the rock or my hollering as the rock pinned both my arms to the cave floor. The dirt and dust fogged up the cave and made the flashlight beam dim through the thick dust.

There was a huge silence. Lee and I held our breath expecting the sound of a loud explosion.

After a few moments, I whispered to Lee. "Can you gently lift these rocks off my arms?" Lee immediately laid the flashlight on the floor and started moving the smaller rocks gently one at a time so not to jar anything else.

Lee was scared, her voice shaky, she said, "Rolf, do you think you have any broken bones; can you feel anything in your hands?"

"I can see some blood running down your left arm; "Oh hell," I hope you're not hurt bad."

"Hey Lee, cool it down, it's just scratched and I don't think I gotten any broken bones; I can move my fingers but my arms hurt from that boulder lying on them."

"Can you get that tire iron under the edge of the rock and raise it a little and I'll see if I can wiggle one of my arms out." Lee shoved the tire iron under the rock and raised the rock just enough to get an arm out; then under the other side, freeing the other arm.

It looked like I had a minor cut and some bruises. I was lucky because a big pointed edge of the rock hit the floor between my arms, taking the weight of the stone rather than crushing my arms.

"I'm OK Lee, grab the flashlight and let's see what we've uncovered." The light penetrated the thick fog of dust.

There in front of us was a stack of gold arm bracelets three feet high. Lee shinned the light around the room as much as she could through the opening in the wall. The room was packed full of gold objects and old wooden boxes.

I took the flashlight from Lee's shaking hand. "I'm going in Lee". Lee grabbed hold of my shoulder saying; "be careful Rolf, this place is probably really booby trapped."

I eased through the opening very carefully so not to knock any more loose rocks down. I moved the flashlight beam around the floor area looking for anything that might be a trip wire. I noticed an old four legged table loaded down with five wooden boxes. I moved closer to the table. I could see the faded writing on the side of the box, "Dynamite."

The legs and the top of the old table were badly rotted where water must have seeped down from the ceiling over the years. I shinned the flashlight into the top dynamite box. The dynamite sticks looked like big reddish-orange candles with a sweaty liquid all over them.

This liquid residue must be the nitro-glycerin Taza was talking about. There is no way of moving that table or the boxes without risking a big boom.

Lee was inching her way through the opening into the room. "Lee", I spoke softly, "there is no way we can move this dynamite out of here, it's just too risky".

Lee replied, "Ya, but we can move the gold into the cave and haul it out and leave the dynamite right where it's at."

"Lee, that's a good thought but one small jar or vibration and we're history."

Lee was already starting to pick up various gold artifacts. "Boy, are these things heavy," Lee exclaimed as she slid a handful of arm bracelets on her arms for carrying them out side.

Bannerstone 103

"Lee, how about you get through the hole to the other side and I'll hand you the artifacts?"

"Sounds like a plan to me," Lee excitedly exclaimed.

I worked my way slowly around the room picking up each item as if it were the last thing I'd ever pick up. I reached up to pick up a leather saddle bag which was lying on a rafter when I spotted a small copper wire attached to the buckle.

"Lee", I shouted, "don't move anything, I think I've found a trip wire and I don't know where it goes so hold tight while I try to run it down."

The wire ran from the buckle up over a rafter and through a hole in the door frame. I carefully moved back to the saddle bag and untied the wire from the buckle and then tied the end of the wire off to a rafter. My hands were shaking like a maple leaf in a strong wind.

I reached up and slowly pulled the saddle bags off the rafter. The bags came fast and hard as they struck my shoulder knocking me back as me and the saddle bags hit the sandstone floor.

I lay on my back clutching the old leather bags afraid to even breathe. I finally got my senses together and rose up sitting flat on the floor.

Lee was outside hollering in hysteria.

"Lee", I shouted, It's Ok, "We're still in one piece."

I picked up the flashlight and slowly unbuckled the bag flaps. I eased up the flap while shinning the beam into the bag.

No wonder it was so darn heavy, it was full of gold nuggets about the size of a dime.

Setting directly below the saddlebags was an old bucket partially covered over with a large piece of leather. I reached down and slowly raised the leather and shinned the flashlight into the bucket.

There was the detonator box with the handle pulled up and two wires running over the side of the bucket.

If someone had opened the door, the trip wire would have pulled the saddlebags off the rafter and fell into the bucket pushing the plunger down on the detonator and setting off the dynamite.

Pretty darn clever, I'd say. I checked the door edge closely where the wire had been attached to the bags. It looked as though they had left just enough slack in the wire so it could be hooked to the door edge when the door was open about an inch. This way they could connect and disconnect it as they used the door. Very simple, but effective way to guard the gold.

I decided I better follow those wires coming out of the bucket and disconnect them from the dynamite. Sure enough, the wires ran over to the table with the boxes of dynamite stacked on it.

After looking the situation over, I decided it would be better to unhook the wires at the detonator instead of moving any thing on that rickety old table.

I felt a sigh of relief when I pulled the last wire from the detonator. I remembered the one stick of dynamite lying on the rock shelf I had seen when we pulled the rock out of the door earlier. I shinned the light towards the top of the wall, and there it was. I eased up to take a better look and it seemed to be lying pretty solid so I'm going to just leave it there.

Lee and I had been carrying out gold for the past three hours and we were beat.

"Lee, lets take a break?" Lee looked up from where she had been stacking the artifacts saying; "I never thought I'd get tired of seeing treasure, but I'm sick of carrying this gold around already."

"Ya Lee, I know what you mean; the excitement of finding riches wears off quickly once reality sets in."

"You know the fun is in the looking, and finding is when the work begins." Lee answered back, "The spending won't exactly be torture either."

"Lee, it's good to have enough money to cover what you need, but not more than what you need, because it's a hassle to have to keep up with it."

"Ya", Lee shrugged her shoulders, "that's why giving this gold to Taza to help them get back to their home makes you feel so darn good."

"You know Lee, we have got to contact Taza and let her know we have recovered the gold."

"Ok", Lee answered, "but tell her it's going to be a couple of hours before we get all the gold out of the room."

We walked out of the cave into the bright sunlight. I reached into my shirt and wrapped my hand around the Bannerstone. It started heating up immediately. I closed my eyes and cleared my head thinking only of what I wanted to ask Taza.

An incoming thought popped into my head. Taza replied, "I'll meet you two in the box canyon at 9:00 pm; "good going." Taza sounded excited and her saying "good going" was like me jumping up and down, flinging my arms and shouting great, wonderful,and fantastic. People from Junlk just don't show much emotion about anything.

"Lee, they'll meet us in the box canyon at 9:00 tonight and Taza sounded excited and said thanks to both of us."

Lee didn't say a word but walked toward me looking down at something she was holding in her hand.

"Rolf, look at this; I found it inside an old pottery jug in there." Lee held the round gold object up to my face so close I couldn't make it out in broad daylight. I reached up and took the round disc. It looked like a gold Olympic medal.

"Lee this medallion has engravings all over it."

"It has three tomahawks around the edge; mountains with streams and a big rock over the top of what looks like a cave."

"It also has some Indian symbols and the sun coming up in the East."

"This has some of the same markings that map you found in the leather skirt you bought in Milo Boles store"! Lee was pushing her head against mine trying to see what I was looking at."

Before I could say another word, Lee snatched the gold disc out of my hand and started studying the fine engraving.

Suddenly, Lee shouted out; "I know what this is; it's a map to the location of the gold mine back in the Carolina's." Lee continued, "Remember what Jack was saying about the three tomahawks that marked the location of the gold mine and this has the three tomahawks on it."

"Ya Lee, I remember the story and even Taza said there was gold there, but they couldn't find the location because of the franklinite in the soil."

"Lee laid her arms on my shoulder saying; "wouldn't it be great to go find that mine?" Then Lee excitedly squealed; "Hell, let's go do it." She had both arms around my neck and jumping up and down.

"Lee, I answered, "we have a lot of things to think about right now." "First things first; we need to break out that picnic basket and have lunch, I'm starving to death."

Lee and I sat on the creek bank on a red and white checkered table cloth Nora had tossed in, along with biscuits, bacon and two fried eggs left over from breakfast.

"Damn these are good," I exclaimed. "I don't think I ever tasted any thing better." Lee agreed as she took a swig of water out of the fruit jar she'd brought drinking water in.

Lee handed me the fruit jar and I took a healthy drink. I don't know why but fruit jar water always smells different but has a great taste.

After we polished off the lunch, Lee slid around on the table cloth and leaned her back against me. We talked about the medallion and discussed what some of the symbols might mean. It was nice just sitting there listening to the slow moving water ripple over the rocks and an occasional leaf finding it's way down the creek, dodging the rocks as it floated out of sight.

"You know Lee; this is where it's at." You can feel God's love, and he intends for us to live in a place like this."

"This feels like we've found it." Lee turned her head around and buried her nose into my neck and said; "Ya, if we don't get back to work moving that gold out and be darn careful about it, we might be scattered all over the place for ever and ever; if you know what I mean."

Thirteen

Lee had a way about her of breaking up a serious moment. "Let's get to it Miss slave driver, wouldn't want that gold to go bad while we were relaxing for a moment."

Lee and I gathered up the table cloth and picnic basket and headed up to the cave opening. The tunnel of the cave was stacked wall to wall with gold artifacts. We worked our way through the pieces to reach the wall opening.

It's hard to imagine those Indians transporting all this gold from the Carolina's to here; it must have taken at least three or four big wagon loads because of the weight of the gold.

Lee and I continued moving artifacts out of the rock walled room to the mine tunnel. "Hey Lee, look at this; it's a musket ball mold and here's a pot full of molded balls and they are solid gold."

"I guess they shoot as good as lead balls."

"When you look at all these artifacts, they're things they used in everyday living."

"The bowls and cups, the big round pots were probably used for storing grain."

"The bracelets and jewelry was probably worn in tribal ceremonies."

Lee spoke up, "I think the jewelry was worn by the women to attract strong young handsome braves to their Teepee's."

"Ya," I said, "I guess some Indian women were vain like some women today, not that I know anyone like that."

Lee made a lunge forward towards me and I jumped backwards

hitting the rotted table loaded with dynamite.

The table screeched and started to fall.

I grabbed the table top edge just as it started to twist and fall down.

I fell to my knees holding the table balanced on the twisted legs. "Don't move or breathe," I spoke in a muffled voice. "Grab the other side of the table Lee, hurry, but gently or we're both history."

Lee moved like a flash to the other side of the table and grabbed the edge. "Now what," she asked?

"I ain't got a clue," I answered, but it better be good."

The dynamite under the table was the unknown. We knew it was there, but we couldn't see it.

"Lee, my side of the table is gone; I can't let go to see underneath."

"Can you bend down and see where that dynamite is at and if we can move the table without disturbing it?"

"Rolf, I've got to let go with one hand to see underneath."

"Ok, I think I've got it balanced." My voice was shaky and my arms were trembling.

"Rolf, I can't see under the table, it's too dark."

"The flashlight is behind you where I dropped it; can you reach it?"

Lee answered," I think so; "ya," I got it."

"Rolf, raise the table about six inches and it will clear the top of the box; the wooden skirt on the table is hanging below the box of dynamite."

"Ok, Lee said, I've got the table with both hands now; let's raise it up together."

We both held our breath while we gently raised the table and moved it sideways till we cleared the boxes of dynamite. Now all we had to do is figure out how to set a four legged table with three legs down without dumping the dynamite off the top.

"Lee, we got a big problem; can you come around to this side of the table and hold it while I lift the dynamite boxes off the top?"

Lee answered back; "you just hold the table and I'll lift the dynamite boxes off the table."

"Ok, but be really careful."

Bannerstone 109

Lee and I eased the three legs down till we felt them all touch the stone floor and felt fairly stable. Lee said; "I'm letting go now; have you got it?"

"Ya, do it", I whispered in a low unsure voice. The table gave a little twist sideways. I gripped the table top with everything I had. It seemed to stabilize.

Lee moved around the box, rubbed her hands together briskly and extended her arms out and gently grabbed hold of both sides of the box. She gave out a grunt as she lifted the first box from the table and slowly rotated to set the box on the floor.

"Lee, get the flashlight and check out that second box before you move it."

The second box stood low enough we could see in it. The nitro sweat covered the red sticks of dynamite like the forehead of a boxer after ten rounds.

Lee grabbed the box and shifted it to the floor.

The last box had a lid nailed down. Lee gently lifted the third box and just as she started to rotate to set it down, the rotted bottom of the box fell out and the contents came crashing onto the table.

Our hearts were in our mouths, we both stood not breathing or moving a muscle. Lee slowly opened her tightly closed eyes to see a horse halter and a pair of old cowboy boots sprawled out on the table.

We both looked at each other and started laughing hysterically. We were so relieved and surprised that we were still alive that we just stood there and laughed like idiots.

Lee looked me directly in the eyes saying, "Rolf, I pissed my pants." She was so serious that I almost fell out laughing.

The look on her face; no one, could have kept a straight face. Lee continued, "I'm not talking dribble, I'm talking flood."

I finally got control of myself and said; "Lee, I'm sorry for laughing and I'm surprised I didn't pee mine."

"I've got a extra pair of jeans in the truck."

"I always carry an extra pair behind the driver's seat ever since I split the rear end out of my britches while I was playing baseball."

"I happened to be the catcher and I played the whole game with my butt showing; so needless to say, I always carry a spare pair."

Lee chirped up, "I remember that game and I never laughed so hard to see you run with the seat of your pants flopping as you went around the bases."

Lee and I both got our stress relief laughs out and boy did we need the relief.

I was still shaky as I let the table down to the floor. The table was so rotten; I don't know how it stood for all those years. I'm just glad the two top boxes were not that rotted.

"Come on Rolf, Lee said, I need to get out of these wet pants, and by the way, you walk in front of me and I'll follow you."

"Don't you think I ever seen a wet pair of britches before," I ask? "No", Lee answered, "not on me."

We walked back to the truck, I opened the door and reached behind the seat and pulled out a dusty pair of Levis. "Here you go Lee; they're a little dusty but their dry."

Lee caught the little smile on my face. "Very, very funny," Lee exclaimed. She grabbed the blue jeans and headed around the other side of the truck. I started to follow.

"Stay", Lee commanded. "I don't need any help."

"I was just going to protect you from snakes and wild varmints while you had your britches down."

"Rolf, the only varmint I have to watch out for is you." Lee laughed with a hearty high pitched voice.

A few minutes past before Lee came back around the truck.

"Hey Lee, you look great in my jeans, especially with the rolled up pant cuffs." I had to laugh but Lee seen no humor in the situation.

"I'm going back to the creek to rinse these clothes out," Lee exclaimed. She took off down the path towards the creek. I walked behind her as she trucked down the creek bank. She filled my jeans out pretty good in the back. That little wiggle when she walked in tight jeans was really cute.

She made her way down the creek bank and found a big flat rock to wash her clothes out.

"Rolf, come here and look at this fish." I walked down the bank to see what Lee had spotted. "Damn, that's a big bass and I'll bet he's got relatives in there too."

Lee turned saying, "This would be a good place to bring a hook and skillet."

"Ya", I said, there ain't nothing better than catchem,cleanem, and cookem right here on the creek bank."

Lee glanced down into the water, "I hate washing these clothes out here, the water is so clear and the fish…." I interrupted, "Lee, I don't think a little pee in the stream will contaminate the water or kill the fish, after all, the creek is the favorite place for a herd of cows to let it fly." Lee looked at me with one eyebrow twisted up saying, "I hope there are no cows up stream right now, and I want to wash pee out of the clothes, not in."

Lee eyed the water for a moment and leaned over the big flat rock and started washing the clothes in the clear cold water. She beat them against the rocks and rinsed them.

"Lee, give me the jeans and I'll wring the water out." Lee handed me the jeans and I twisted them tight till the water quit running out of them. "There's a tree up on the bank with some low limbs, I'll hang them there to dry."

Lee had made it up the bank with panties in hand and found a limb to hang them over.

We went back to the cave to finish getting the last of the artifacts out of the room. The sandstone floor was fairly empty except for the dynamite boxes, the old table and some long poles leaning against the side wall. We cleaned up the remaining items around the wooden door.

"Rolf, why don't we open the door and get some more light in here."

"Hey, that's a great idea Lee, wonder why I didn't think of that?"

I moved over to the heavy wooden door and grabbed hold of the thick timbers and give a big jerk. The door moved open dragging on the sandstone floor as I tugged and pulled the door open. I moved the sandstone blocks away that had hid the door on the outside. The majority of the sandstone blocks were only six inches thick but they really did the job of hiding the doorway. The room lit up with sunlight. We slowly walked around the room looking for any more booby traps because as clever as they were, we knew they were capable of setting some unique traps.

In the back wall about five feet over from where we had cut the hole in the wall were four round holes about two inches in diameter.

I shinned the flashlight beam into the holes as far as possible but couldn't see anything. The holes seemed really deep.

"Lee, what do you think these holes were used for?"

Lee looked carefully at the holes and then started looking around the floor. Lee reached down and picked four pieces of small round sandstone rocks and started pushing one in each hole.

"These holes were plugged with these sandstone plugs to hide them," Lee exclaimed.

Lee continued, "We need something to stick in the holes to see how deep they are."

"How about those long poles over there against the wall," I commented; "they are about the right size to fit those holes."

I picked up one of the poles and placed the end into the hole. It fit perfectly. I pushed the six foot pole in about five feet and it hit something but I could tell it wasn't rock. I gently tapped the pole against the object and it seemed to have a sound like possibly a clay pot.

I drew the pole back and rammed it as hard as I could into the hole. I heard a crash breaking sound and then the pouring of sand and dust bellowed out of the hole. I ran over to the other wall and picked up the remaining three poles. I rammed each one in the other three holes and each time I heard a clay pot break and the pouring of sand.

As the sound of the pouring sand resonated through the wall, a large screeching sound started. Lee and I looked up next to the ceiling where a two foot wide section of the wall started moving down creating a gap which was widening at the top of the wall.

It was a small doorway opening up. "Well I'll be damned," I said, "the Egyptians used the same method for sealing their tombs in the Pyramids and the Indians used it to open a secret passage."

"The Egyptians put these below each sliding rock door and they filled the cavity with sand and in the bottom of cavity they put a clay pot in the hole to hold the sand from running out."

"When the pots were broken, the sand ran out and the rock door moved down and sealed the interior of the pyramid."

"That is really genius", Lee exclaimed, "what a neat way to hide a secret passage."

The rock continued to slide down until there was an opening about

Bannerstone 113

three feet high and then came to a sudden stop.

"Lee, let me lift you up to see in the opening."

I tried to lift Lee but I couldn't lift her high enough. "Lee, I'll bend down and you straddle my neck and I'll lift you that way."

"Ok", Lee said in excitement. "Here's the flashlight, up we go."

I lifted Lee easily to the opening. Lee shined the light into the opening.

"Holy Shit," she hollered out, "it's full of gold and silver bars and gold coins." Lee reached in grabbing a hand full of gold coins."

"Look at these," Lee shouted. "There must be a million dollars worth of coins in here."

I bent down and Lee crawled off from around my neck. "Let's take these out side so we can see them better," Lee shrieked. She went tearing out the door to the bright sunlight.

"Lee, these are Mexican coins."

"How did the Indians end up with Mexican gold coins," Lee questioned?

I remember reading in one of those treasure magazines about a wagon load of gold and silver vanished in Kansas during the Civil War while it was being moved from Mexico to Virginia."

"Lee, we are more than just rich, we are filthy rich."

Lee stood silent for a moment as in deep thought and then said, "Rolf, who does this gold and silver belong to; is it the Indians, the Watson's or the Government or the one who finds it?"

Lee continued, "Why don't we ask Taza's opinion?"

"That's a good idea Lee." I reached inside my shirt and grabbed hold of the Bannerstone. It warmed and she immediately answered saying; "We must move all the items away from the area as soon as possible for many reasons."

"Possession is the primary importance and she will meet us tonight as planned and discuss details."

The Bannerstone started to cool; I knew that was the end of that conversation.

Lee questioned," What did she say?"

"She just said hold tight till tonight and we'll discuss it."

"Well, Lee said, "We won't have too long to wait because the sun is starting to set and it'll be dark in about an hour and it'll be 9:00

before you know it."

Lee and I went back inside the cabin because I had to get a look at all that gold and silver. I went over to the back wall and stood below the opening. It was too high for me to see in so I pulled the old table over next to the wall while Lee steadied it; I crawled up and stood on the edge and shined the flashlight beam into the opening.

It was breath taking to see all the stacks of gold and silver bars and the sacks of gold coins which had rotted and spilled coins all over the area.

The little room was really unique. It was carved out of solid sandstone and was about three feet high and about four feet wide and probably ten feet deep and was packed with treasure. I grabbed a handful of coins so I could show Taza what we had found.

Lee and I walked up and around the big rocks to get a view of the setting sun in the west. It was a beautiful evening; the sky had a gold background which lit up the reds and blues, purple and pink clouds. We sat on a big flat sandstone rock which protruded out of the prairie grass like a giant mushroom.

We started talking about all the happenings of the day and boy was it ever an exciting day. I reached in my pocket and pulled out one of the gold coins. Lee asked, "Tell me more about that article you read about the vanished wagon load of gold."

I began, "Well, the article said that during the civil war the North needed gold and silver to trade to France and some other European countries for Guns, Cannons, supplies and to meet their own Army payroll."

"The North made a secret agreement with Mexico that it would sell them what is now, Arizona and Southern part of California, these territories for some large amount of gold and silver."

"The North sent a fifty man Calvary to Mexico to escort the five wagon loads of gold and silver back to Virginia."

"Well, they got into fights with different tribes of Indians on the way back."

"The Indians would signal ahead and every attack, more soldiers were killed."

"They fought their way through Texas, Oklahoma and Kansas Territory following the Santa Fe and Chisholm Trail and ended up on the Oxhide Trail going towards Kansas City."

"One night, a heavy rain storm hit and during the storm, one of the wagons was unloaded of all its gold and silver and no one knew it till next morning."

"The only clue was they found hoof prints of a lot of horses in one area but couldn't follow them because the rain had washed out the tracks."

"None of the horses had horseshoes so they figured it was some renegade Indians who had stolen the gold and silver."

"They needed to get the remaining four wagon loads to Kansas City and then on to Virginia soon as possible so they didn't spend a lot of time trying to track down the renegade Indians."

"No one ever heard of the whereabouts of the wagon load of gold and silver."

"Some said that Missouri Border Ruffians got it; others say the Mexican Government followed the wagons and stole it back."

"It was even rumored that some of the troops themselves stole it and hid it."

"The article went on to say that the other four wagons never got to Virginia."

"They disappeared somewhere in the middle of Virginia and have never been found."

"There were some clues and a map left behind but no one has been able to break the code."

"At least there was a clue concerning the four wagons but not a clue of what ever happened to the fifth wagon."

"Rolf, do you think that this is the fifth wagon load?"

"All I know Lee, it sure does fit the amount of gold and silver and the fact it disappeared off the Oxhide trail and that they thought it was Indians who took it; it really fits."

The sun had dropped below the horizon and it was getting dark fast. "No moon tonight," I remarked to Lee while we made our way back to the cabin.

"Wait here Rolf; I've got to get my clothes off the tree limbs while I can still see." Lee hurried down the path toward the creek. She was back in a flash with clothes in hand. "Boy is it ever spooky down next to the creek when it gets dark," Lee exclaimed.

"Ya, there's all kinds of night animals that run about now."

"Coons, Possum, Fox, Wolves, Deer and Coyote; they all like to run at night and this area is full of them because of the cover and the water."

When we got to the truck, Lee informed me that she was going to change clothes on the other side of the truck. I could hear her struggling to get out of my jeans. "Lee, it works best if you unzip the jeans before you try taking them off."

"Very funny Rolf, I think these darn jeans of mine shrunk; I can hardly get into them."

"Ya, I know the feeling; I've had the same problem."

"It's hard to get into your jeans."

Lee answered back quickly, "Boy, are you a comedian tonight."

Lee continued, "I hope finding treasure doesn't make you too horney because we have to meet Taza in about fifteen minutes and you know how she picks up on everything."

"Lee, I promise I'll keep everything concealed." I had to laugh a little under my breath; Lee was on a roll tonight.

We decided to leave the truck sit and walk to the back of the canyon.

It's a good thing this flashlight is holding up. The sky had turned pitch black and no moon tonight was right. We sat down on a rock ledge near the trickling spring that ran out of the box canyon wall.

Chapter fourteen

Lee grabbed me by arm, "look there, a tiny blue light." It was Taza. The craft approached, totally silent and this was a different looking craft then I had witnessed before. It was much smaller and lacked the whale shaped rim around it. It seemed to be boxier. The craft hovered above the ground while three legs extended out of the bottom and stabilized the craft. I could hear a small hum from the craft. Then the center tube moved down to touch the ground and rotated open; Taza stepped out. I'm amazed every time I see this.

Lee still had a death grip on my arm. "It's Ok Lee; you can relax your grip." Lee and I walked out to meet Taza.

I gave Taza a big hug and she held the hug for a seemly long time. Then she hugged Lee the same.

"Taza, I began, we've got more than just the Indian gold; we also uncovered a secret room that is loaded with Mexican gold and silver."

Taza clinched her lips together saying," That explains the reason we were detecting the silver element on our scan of the cabin and we couldn't determine its origin."

"Mexican silver," Taza repeated," I'll research that when I return to the mining module."

"Is this what you call this craft, Lee asked?" Taza pointed toward the craft saying, "yes, it acts as a landing craft for rough terrain and is fitted with loading equipment and a cargo storage area." Taza continued, "Our mother ship has a number of these crafts on board as we utilize these in our mining exploration on large planets."

Taza, Lee and I walked to the cargo door which had just opened. The bright blue light in the interior exposed a platform about four feet square with a control pedestal in the center. Taza motioned for us to step onto the platform.

Our shoes stuck to the surface as if we had been sucked down to the platform by vacuum. Taza laid her hand on a flat glass and the platform module raised and moved out the open cargo bay door moving about a foot off the ground and moving toward the truck.

Taza asked if we needed anything from the truck. I answered, "no, but I only have this flashlight and the batteries are getting a little weak." Taza smiled; reached into a small compartment in the control pedestal and pulled out three pairs of glasses. "These will be all you need."

Lee and I put the glasses on. Every thing looked like midday with the sun shinning. Where ever I looked it was like daytime. There was no light beam shinning or anything.

Lee spoke up, "these are the coolest things I've ever seen." Taza turned to Lee saying, "These are supposed to adjust to your body temperature; do you wish to try another pair?"

"No, no, I mean they are really unique." Lee was totally blown out by the glasses and kept asking how they worked and all kinds of questions.

Taza answered, "The lenses are really cameras, and they take thousands of images per mili-second and expose an image to your eye in daytime color."

Lee and I didn't ask anymore questions about the glasses, needless to say.

We arrived at the cave entrance where Taza parked the module and we proceeded into the cave entrance. We made our way through the artifacts. Taza stopped to pick up some of the engraved gold artifacts saying, "These are unique style engravings with various cosmic signs and shapes utilized; these will be interesting to research." Taza was excited, I could tell by her tone of voice and the way she was admiring everything she walked past.

"I'm amazed", she said, "how the ancients formed all these beautiful designs on artifacts with just simple hand working tools; even the water jugs are decorated and inscribed."

Bannerstone

"We have lost this talent and must rely on machines to perform the artful tasks." She was almost saddened by the beauty of the artifacts, maybe because she knew they would be melted down into whatever they needed for their ships engine drives.

Taza began, "we must vacate this cave and room of all items as if nothing had ever been here; as our findings here never existed."

"Also no record or mention of these findings ever to be disclosed."

"Our crew of workers will remove everything from the premises and seal the cave."

"We will deliver the Mexican gold and silver to your garage behind your house and it will be buried in a secure metal bunker below the existing garage."

"This bunker may be opened by your index finger prints simultaneously on the lock."

"Taza, Lee asked, "Why don't you take the Mexican gold, the silver is all we'll ever need?" Taza looked Lee with an almost tearful look, saying, "Lee, we appreciate your generous offer but the Mexican gold hasn't the molecular structure we need, only the Carolina gold has those properties."

"Rolf, Taza continued," You and Lee must leave now, go back to your house." Taza smiled, saying, "Rolf, don't park your truck in front of your garage tonight." I answered back laughing, "I'll make it a point not to obstruct progress."

We stepped onto the platform and Taza had us back to the truck in a few minutes.

"What about the dynamite," I asked Taza? She answered with out hesitation, "now that we can get to the dynamite, we can extract the explosive elements and use those ingredients in our laboratory on board our ship." Taza continued, "I'll contact you later tonight and inform you of our progress."

Lee and I stepped off the platform. Taza held out her hand saying, "I'll need those glasses; everything must be accounted for when we visit Earth."

"No evidence must be left behind that indicates a more advanced civilization has been here and not only that, you'd have a very hard time explaining where you purchased these glasses and you don't need the problems associated with that."

Taza stepped off the platform and put both arms around Lee and gave her a big hug saying, "God speed." She turned to me and we held each other tightly not saying a word. Then Taza whispered, "We'll be returning home to Junlk and as we speak our crew have been removing the gold from the cave and being loaded aboard ship."

"The first pieces are already being processed in our Laboratory for use in our drive systems."

"Taza, I ask, are you that efficient at everything you do." Taza answered, "we're not very patient but we've found that to be a positive attribute; we utilize time and treat it as a precious commodity and as your technology advances here on Earth, so will your appreciation of how fragile life and the existence of your planet really becomes, therefore time will become a precious thing and you'll want to utilize it effectively."

"When will I see you again Taza", I asked? She looked me directly in the eyes, "you may contact me at anytime, wear the Bannerstone and use it's power wisely; we will meet again in the near future; our people are indebted to you and thank you, both of you." Taza leaned over and kissed me on the cheek. She boarded the platform and was gone in a few seconds.

Lee took hold of my hand, not saying a word. "Lee, Lets head back to the house, I'm starving."

The night was black as tar and the headlights on the truck didn't seem very bright. Jack rabbits were running tonight; all across and down the road. Don't know why they like to run down the middle of the road, maybe they feel safe from the coyotes because coyotes don't like to hang around roads as they have been shot at from pickup trucks too many times.

Lee and I talked all the way back home about all the things that happened today and also trying to figure how the Mexican gold and silver was going to get buried under the garage. It seems a little far fetched to both of us but, we'll see.

I parked the truck about forty five feet from the front of the garage. I wanted to give them plenty of room to work.

Lee and I went inside and headed straight for the kitchen. We found some ham and cheese and a loaf of sourdough bread Nora had baked

Bannerstone 121

and we pigged out. Lee made a pot of coffee and we sat around the table snacking on the fresh baked bread.

"Make a guess what I have in my pocket," Lee asked? "Mexican gold coins," I answered immediately. "No, Lee shook her head, "I put all of those back like we were supposed to do; remember, no trace."

"Ya, I remembered, but I didn't know about you?" Lee pulled the gold medallion from her pocket. I had completely forgotten about the medallion. "Do you think this is a map showing the Indian tribal gold mine," Lee asked? "Well Lee, it sure does have the three tomahawks, the seven springs and a cave below a big rock ledge and that matches Jack's story of where the gold was hidden."

"Lee, it could be it's not the tribal gold mine where they actually dug the gold."

"These could have been two different locations or it could be, they hid the gold in the gold mine." Lee was silent and then spoke," There's only one way to find out."

"Ya, I know Lee but it's a long trip to the Carolina's and right now, I'm beat and ready for bed."

Lee agreed, sticking the medallion back in her tight jean pocket.

"I turned to Lee saying, "I think we've got about all we can get out of this day." Lee hesitated at her bedroom door, "Rolf come here;" she spoke in a commanding tone of voice. I walked over to see what she had thought of now. She put both arms around my neck and pulled me close to her and gently pressed her lips to mine and whispered, "Good night and sweet dreams." She spun on her heels and into her bedroom closing the door behind her.

"WOW", did I ever want to open that door and slide in bed with her but I bit my lip and went on down the hall to my bedroom.

I woke abruptly, sitting up in bed; the Bannerstone was hot against my chest. I reached wrapping my fingers around it. It was Taza. She started off with, "Mission successfully completed." She had a happy almost musical sound in her voice. She went on to say, "Your Mexican gold and silver has been placed below the garage floor and the access controller is located inside the garage in the left rear corner."

"Simply lift the left side of the short wood two by four, exposing the keypad of the finger print security lock."

"Both you and Lee must press your index fingers on the pad at the same time."

"A section of concrete floor will rise exposing a staircase."

"We have compacted the soil similar to the cave wall, so don't be concerned with any type of soil cave-in."

"At the bottom of the stairs is a wall vault constructed of Inconel steel."

"Again, with a finger print security lock requiring both you and Lee's print simultaneously."

"Inside lays the Mexican gold and silver bars, the gold coins and a small token of our appreciation."

"Rolf, my love for you is eternal, but we have different destinies and responsibilities, each with our own people."

"My love will always be with you; our work will be our destiny." The Bannerstone started to cool and I knew Taza was on her way home.

I looked at the clock on the dresser table; it was 5:00 AM. I couldn't wait; I had to see this vault under the garage. I jumped out of bed, into my pants and shirt and slid my boots on, and ran down the hall to Lee's room. I didn't want to knock on the door afraid of waking Nora so I eased the door open and closed it quietly behind me. Lee was lying with a thin sheet covering her shapely body. She's quite the beautiful woman I must admit.

I reached down gently and touched Lee's shoulder. She jumped straight up in bed, grabbing at covers to pull up over her bare breasts. It was good that the room was pretty dark so I could tell her I didn't see a thing. "Lee", I whispered, "Taza just contacted me and said everything went as planned."

"Get up and get dressed, we've got to go out to the garage." Lee slid out from under the sheet, naked as a new hatched bird and started putting on her clothes. "Lee, I gasp, it's not that dark in here." Lee looked up saying, "I didn't mean to shock you, but I want to see the garage."

"Rolf, if there's something you don't want to see, close your eyes."

I was totally taken back by Lee's lack of modesty. I just wasn't used to someone being that open about things. I couldn't keep from thinking that Lee is definitely "one of a kind" girl as she hopped

Bannerstone 123

around on one foot trying to get her other shoe on.

"Let's go Rolf; I can't wait to get out there." On the way to the garage I told Lee everything Taza had said. Naturally, Lee got hung up on how a finger print was going to open anything. I just told her I didn't have the foggiest idea of how it worked.

We entered the side door of the garage, walked to the back left hand corner. I tried to raise the first short two by four but it was securely nailed down. I tried the second one and the left end pivoted up. There was a round glass that looked like the end of a telescope. Lee and I took our index fingers and pressed them against the glass.

Immediately, a three foot by four foot section of concrete floor started to tilt and one end pivoted up exposing a stairway. I started down with Lee right on my heels. We reached the bottom of the stairs and there in front of us was a full wall covered by shiny steel. All four walls were the same. Each wall had a finger print lock. Lee and I placed our index fingers on the wall lock in front of us and a wall panel slid down flush with the floor.

The compartment had many shelves each stacked with gold and silver bars, but on the middle shelf there was nothing but a lone velvet bag. The bag stood approximately eight inches high and about eight inches around and a note sticking out from under the bag.

I reached in and opened the top of the bag and out spilled beautiful sparkling diamonds.

Lee and I stood in utter shock and amazement. Neither of us could speak, we were totally breathless. Lee finally caught her breath and carefully pulled the paper from under the bag.

Lee unfolded the note and started to read aloud. "Rolf and Lee: in appreciation for your generosity, and a token of our friendship, Love to you both and Gods Blessing."

I had a lump in my throat the size of a baseball but finally managed to speak. "Lee, there must be millions of dollars worth of diamonds here?" I picked up one large oval shaped diamond about the size of a robin's egg. It was absolutely beautifully cut. The stone looked like it was on fire with all the colors reflecting out of it. Lee was fingering through the bag admiring each different shape and cut of diamonds.

"Lee, it looks like we've got our own private Fort Knox here and no one knows we have it."

"Ya Rolf and we'll have to be so careful not to ever let anyone find out about it or even suspect us of having these riches."

"We've got a lot of homework to do," I commented, "and it's not going to be easy because this kind of wealth brings a lot of responsibility and a real challenge to always do the right thing."

"Knowing first hand that giving is much more rewarding than receiving, but giving without hurting someone becomes a tough judgment call."

Lee spoke up, "I know of two different people who their parents passed away and left the family farm to them, and they didn't have the farm a year and they sold it."

"They took the money and blew it gambling and drinking and raising hell and one of them ended up behind bars."

"Ya Lee, it ain't going to be easy but Taza had faith in us that we could handle it or she wouldn't have given it to us."

"You are absolutely right Rolf and I think we can have a lot of fun at this and do a lot of good for a lot of people."

Lee continued, "This is a good place to leave this gold medallion; it's been worrying me that someone might see it and ask where I got it."

She reached into her jean pocket and placed the medallion beside the velvet bag of diamonds. We gathered up all the diamonds that had spilled out and closed the bag.

Lee and I stepped back from the wall and pressed a small flashing blue light button. The wall panel started moving up sealing the entire wall. We exited up the stairs and hit the flashing blue button on the controller and returned the two by four to the original position. The concrete floor section pivoted down flat to the floor.

There was no way of telling the floor section had ever moved.

"Lee, I asked, "what do you think about going back out to the old cabin after breakfast and see how Taza left things?"

"Great", Lee answered, and it'll give us some private time to talk about what we want to do next."

Nora was already up and fixing breakfast. She looked surprised when we opened the kitchen door. "I thought you two were still asleep upstairs; where in the world have been?"

Lee answered, "Oh, we woke up early and went for a walk down

Bannerstone 125

the old field road to see how the wheat was coming along."

"If we don't get a huge wind storm, Rolf said he might get the biggest wheat crop they've had in years."

I changed the subject fast because I could see by the expression on Nora's face she wasn't buying what Lee said because Lee didn't normally show much interest if a wheat crop was ever good or bad.

"How is the new house coming Nora," I asked? Nora turned with a somewhat discussed look saying, "Since they started on finishing the inside, they have been slower than Christmas and I can't believe it takes so long to put up trim and paint some walls; I swear I think their painting with one hair in their paint brushes."

"You know if you need some help painting, I'd be glad to help and I know I've got a paint brush with at least two hair bristles in it." Nora cracked a little smile.

"Ya Mom, I can help paint," Lee commented. Nora turned to Lee, "What has happened to you that you would volunteer painting?" Lee came back with a smug look on her face, "Just maybe I am maturing and want to take on responsibilities." Nora threw up both hands, "Glory", the day has finally come, wait till I tell your daddy or better yet, I better wait till after breakfast before I tell him, I'd hate for him to die of shock before he's had breakfast."

I had never heard Nora laugh so loud at a joke, even one of her own.

"I really do appreciate you both offering to paint but we've contracted the painting out to a fellow out of Lyons and he's doing a good job, he's just slow."

Charlie had heard all the laughter and had come in to see what was going on. Charlie came into the kitchen stretching and yawning and half asleep, saying, "I suppose you all know you're making enough noise to wake the whole neighborhood; don't know how anyone could have that much fun this early in the morning?" Charlie pulled out a chair and sat down at the table.

"What'd you find out at the old Watson cabin yesterday," Charlie asked, "is it still standing?"

"Sure is", I answered, "the roof has fell in some and vines and weeds have pretty well taken over, but it's still standing."

Charlie came back, "I figured it would still be there, being made out of sandstone rock."

Nora and Lee started setting the table with a platter of eggs, sausage and a big bowl of gravy. Lee placed a plate of biscuits in front of me saying, "Now if you had all the money in the world, do you think you could buy a better breakfast?" I looked up at Lee and smiled saying, "no and I couldn't find a better waitress either."

After breakfast, Nora and Charlie left the house to check on the contractor's progress. Lee and I jumped in the truck and took off for the box canyon to check out the cabin.

We pulled into the canyon entrance. "Rolf, Let's park here and walk into the canyon."

"Sure Lee", I answered, "If you're game, I am."

I parked the truck and we strolled leisurely down the dusty road toward the back of the canyon. It was a beautiful morning and the sky was totally clear, not a cloud in the sky. A lone turkey buzzard circled high in the sky and gliding along the canyon rim catching the up draft of the wind currents.

Lee and I walked hand in hand around the canyon and down the path to the old cabin.

We pushed open the door, it dragged on the sandstone floor making its same weird noise; we walked inside. There was a warm peaceful feeling about the place although it looked exactly like we had found it. I think us knowing what went on here has given us a sense of familiarity that makes it feel like an old friend.

We left the cabin and followed the path that led to the creek. Lee hurried ahead of me, she was anxious to see the cave. Lee walked right past where the cave entrance used to be. There was not any indication that there had ever been a cave there. Even the dead tree branches and leaves looked to be undisturbed. We even checked the bluff area above the cave entrance and there wasn't a clue that would indicate that any one had been there.

"Lee, you know it is amazing technology those people possess." Lee laid her hand on my shoulder, "Do you think we'll have spacecraft in our lifetime that can take us to other planets?"

"Maybe", I answered, "if we live long enough, but we're a long, long way from that capability now."

From the top of the bluff, Lee and I looked out over the prairie grass blowing in the wind like ocean waves. "Lee, you know it just don't get any better than this."

"Ya, Lee said, but there is one thing we need to do." I was almost afraid to ask what, knowing Lee, but I thought I might as well be brave.

I answered, "What Lee?" She came back quickly, "we need to just leave that gold and silver where it is and take a few of the smaller diamonds and cash them in."

"Then go to the North Carolina Blue Ridge Mountains to see if that gold mine exists." I thought for a moment, "Hell yes, let's do it."

THE END

ISBN 1425137b7-9